SOUTHERN ANGELS

# HEARTS DIVIDED

CHERYL ZACH

For Gary,
Very best wishes —
Cheryl Zach

This book is dedicated, with much love, to my mother, Nancy LeGate Byrd, and my father, Smith Henry Byrd, and their parents and grandparents and all the generations of  Southerners before them, including, according to family lore, the ancestors who fought on both sides of the Civil War

Four Southern girls: Elizabeth Stafford of Virginia, Victoria LaGrande of New Orleans, the slave Hannah, Rosamund Brigham of Tennessee, all about to face America's most tumultuous era. Three of the girls attend a boarding school in Charleston, South Carolina as the state votes to secede from the Union. Hannah, who grew up with Elizabeth on her plantation, now works in a nearby shop. Just as all four step into adulthood, their country will be divided. Can the girls' friendships survive when loyalties are torn asunder? Can love find a way through the uncertainty and dangers of war?

SOUTHERN ANGELS
by Cheryl Zach
Book 1: Hearts Divided
Book 2: Winds of Change
Book 3: A Dream of Freedom
Book 4: Last Rebellion
In paper and e-book format, order from your bookstore or on
Amazon.com

*"Readers will be caught up in the drama and watch Elizabeth grow from a flirty teenager into an independent-thinking woman capable of making valuable contributions . . . a quick read with dramatic action and memorable characters. . ."*

*School Library Journal*

Hearts Divided is a VRW Holt Medallion winner.

Cheryl Zach also writes Regency historical adventure for adults as Nicole Byrd:

The Sinclair saga:

*Dear Imposter*

*Beauty in Black*

*Vision in Blue*

*Lady in Waiting*, and more–
see www.cherylzach.com

# Chapter One
### Charleston: December 19, 1860

"He'll come," Elizabeth Stafford predicted, laughing. "He promised me."

Pushing a strand of chestnut hair back from her forehead, she strained to see more clearly in the dark garden. The moon had slipped behind a cloud. She could make out only bare tree branches and through their black silhouettes, an occasional star twinkling in the December sky. The air was cold and damp, but Elizabeth didn't mind.

"How will he get over the wall?" Rosamund Brigham tugged her wide hoop skirt away from the thorny clutches of a rose bush. "He'll get hurt. I don't know how you laugh about it, Elizabeth. Don't you have any feelings?"

"*Mais non*," Victorine LaGrande answered before Elizabeth could say a word. She giggled. "Elizabeth has no heart. Did you not know that?" Pulling her shawl more closely around her, she shivered. "Anyhow, I'm cold. I think we should go in."

"You're always cold." Rosamund shook her blonde head. "Perhaps we should send you back to New Orleans, that is, if Madame Corday doesn't send you there first. We'll all be in dreadful trouble if Madame catches us out here at this hour. I'm sure she'd say it's not very ladylike."

"Who wants to be a lady?" Elizabeth drew a deep breath and felt her stays cut into her ribs. Sometimes she wished she could be a little girl again, with no constraining corsets, bothersome hoops, or long skirts.

"Elizabeth!" Victorine frowned.

But Elizabeth's patience, never her strongest point, was wearing thin. They had waited almost an hour, and still there was no sound from beyond the wall, no indication that her suitor, Stephan Hall, would soon make an appearance.

Elizabeth knew they must be a strange sight, the three of them huddled in the dark, winter-bare garden. The moon emerged from its blanket of clouds, and she glanced back to look at her friends: blonde, blue-eyed Rosamund, medium in height and more shapely than Elizabeth; and petite, dark-haired Victorine, shivering in her elegant dress and thick shawl. Elizabeth herself was tall for a girl and willowy, with deep green eyes and unruly reddish-brown hair.

"Ya'll needn't worry," she said, stubborn as usual. "If we get caught, Madame will know who to blame. It will be my fault, as always." She crouched lower. "Hush! I hear something."

But it was only the wind, shaking the bare trees. Elizabeth glanced at the handsome white frame mansion behind them. Was that a light in Madame Corday's bedroom? Her pulse quickened.

"We should go in," Rosamund urged, as if reading her friend's thoughts.

"I won't!" Disappointment made Elizabeth irritable. "I'm not leaving until he comes. I've bet Victorine my best corset-cover—"

"The one trimmed with blue ribbons and pink rosebud embroidery," Victorine interrupted, her strong Creole accent coloring her words.

"Stephen will come, and he'll climb over the wall," Elizabeth said. "I dared him, and he won't back down. Just wait."

Despite her defiant words, Elizabeth glanced at the house again. She didn't want to get caught by their teacher and sent home in disgrace. Even though she'd been angry at her father's abrupt decision to send her away, she had come to love the boarding school, Madame Corday herself, and her new friends, Rosamund and Victorine. Wall or no, in some ways, she had more freedom here than on her Virginia plantation. . .

"I hear something, too," Rosamund whispered.

Elizabeth's thoughts jerked back to her current position. She strained to hear the soft sounds beyond the fence.

"Miss Elizabeth?" a male voice called softly. "Are you there?"

Elizabeth ran across the grass and placed her cheek against the cold, grainy brick. "Mr. Hall? I'm right here. Can you make it over?"

"Of course! What's one brick wall?"

She smiled to hear the artless confidence in his tone. In some ways, Stephen seemed younger than she. In fact, at nineteen, he was three years older.

"It's an awfully high wall," she pointed out, unable to stop teasing.

"It's nothing. The honor of the college is at stake. Stand away, I'm coming over. Hold that ladder still," he directed someone on the other side.

Elizabeth heard scrambling noises. Moving a little ways back, she stared upward,

catching a glimpse of blond hair and a familiar face pale in the darkness. Then she heard a sudden inhalation of breath.

"Ouch!"

"What's wrong?" she called.

"I've cut my hand. There are broken bottles up here." He seemed so surprised and indignant that Elizabeth's ready laughter overflowed once more.

"Maybe you're not the first gentleman to take a dare?" she guessed.

"It's not a matter for jesting. I'm bleeding, Elizabeth." He sounded like a sulky boy, all his confidence flown.

Elizabeth tried to feel sympathetic, but she had to swallow her giggles. "Is it bad, Stephen?"

"I've spotted my cuff," he told her sternly. "I've got to go and bind this up. I'll talk to you tomorrow after my classes."

"I'll see you tomorrow night at the Christmas ball, silly," she reminded him.

"If I'm well enough to attend."

He sounded so healthy and full of energy that it was hard to take his petulance seriously.

"Of course," Elizabeth muttered, listening to the soft thump as he jumped down. There was a scrape as the ladder was removed, a murmur of conversation, then the sounds faded. She ran back to her friends, still waiting in the cover of the shrubbery.

"What happened?"

"He fought with a broken bottle, and the bottle won. If Stephen ever goes to war, he'll withdraw the first time he gets a drop of blood on his uniform," she told them blithely. "If all of our brave troops are so easily discouraged, I fear for South Carolina."

"He cut himself?" Rosamund sounded alarmed. " Oh, Elizabeth, you are a wretch."

"No one told me there was broken glass on top of the wall," Elizabeth argued. "I didn't know Madame Corday was so tricky."

"Perhaps she knew you were, eh?" Victorine giggled.

Elizabeth made a face.

"So, Stephen did not climb over the wall, and you owe me the corset-cover," Victorine added, her tone now practical. "Now let's go in. My feet are frozen."

"But he came, just as I said he would," Elizabeth repeated. She followed her friends as they hurried back into the side door of the big mansion that housed Madame Corday's Select Academy for Young Ladies.

*Stephen paid heed to my wishes*, Elizabeth thought grimly. *That should count for something*! Her father's usual harsh expression flashed into her mind, his features set sternly. She felt the usual frustration, the old feeling of helplessness. Stephen had come to the wall, even though he hadn't made it over. That showed he cared, didn't it?

So why did she feel such a lingering emptiness inside her?

"Mornin's flown, Miss Elizabeth," Fanny said, her kerchiefed head bent over the tray.

"Here's your tea and some nice hot corn cakes Cook just this minute took off the coals. And I put honey on'em, just the way you like'em."

Elizabeth opened one eye, saw sunlight flooding her airy, high ceilinged bedroom, sighed, and closed it again. "It's too early," she muttered. So much for moonlight adventures.

"It's past eight." Fanny's chocolate-colored oval face showed disapproval. "Now, you get yourself out of bed, Miss Elizabeth, or Madame will scold"

None of the students cared to face Madame's scoldings. Elizabeth sat up, took a quick bite of the warm, fragrant corn cake, and felt for her dressing gown.

Looking across the room, she saw the other bed was empty. Rosamund was already up. But her friend was still a farm girl at heart, Elizabeth told herself. Maybe she enjoyed getting up early.

Between yawns, Elizabeth gulped down her tea, then slipped down from the high bed and headed for the dressing table with its china pitcher and bowl. She poured a little water from the ewer into the big, flowered bowl and reached for the rose-scented soap.

Later, pulling on her second-best corset cover–she had already handed over her best one to Victorine the night before–stepping into her hoop and adjusting her tapes and bows, Elizabeth thought with pleasure of the day ahead.

Tonight was the annual Christmas ball, held before the local girls left school to spend the holidays with their families. Elizabeth would wear the new green satin gown she had cajoled out of her father. A pretty penny it had cost, too, if little enough reward for her first Christmas away from home. Yet, although she missed her beloved Virginia plantation, home had increasingly become a painful place. Never an indulgent parent, her father of late had seemed more and more determined to force Elizabeth into a mold–one into which she feared she would never fit. Sending her off to boarding school was his final attempt to make her into a proper Southern lady.

Dreading this new ordeal, Elizabeth had instead found something different at the Academy. Along with dance steps and fancy needlework, Madame Corday taught them about the world of books and ideas.

Smiling, Elizabeth looked around her. The sun was shining, and there was a party to attend. No bad memories this morning.

She heard a rustle of silk from across the hall. Elizabeth paused in the doorway and looked into Victorine's bedroom. It was a smaller room, but Victorine was its only occupant. Monsieur LaGrande had insisted that his daughter not have a roommate. All the other students agreed that the petite beauty from New Orleans was definitely pampered.

As Elizabeth watched, keeping her thoughts to herself, Victorine adjusted her petticoats and reached for a striped day gown. Patting a dark curl into place, she looked up and smiled.

"Would you help me do up these buttons, Elizabeth, *s'il vous plait*? I wish Madame would allow us to have our own maids."

Elizabeth walked into the bedroom and pushed the long line of tiny ivory buttons into their buttonholes.

Victorine smiled over her shoulder. "I cannot wait for the ball tonight, *non?*"

"Yes," Elizabeth agreed. "I'm tired of studying. I'm still trying to understand that long work by Mr. Darwin."

"*Moi aussi,*" Victorine agreed. "Literature and history, philosophy and science. *Mon dieu*, I was expecting to learn only new embroidery stitches when I came here."

Elizabeth laughed. "That's not Madame's style, and you know it. Anyone who attended the Parisian salons and listened to Mr. Dickens lecture would certainly teach more than just needlework and etiquette."

Victorine's pretty mouth drooped. "I think my poor brain has had more exertion since I came to Charleston than it had in my whole life before."

"I can believe that." Elizabeth tried to hide her smile. "There, you're finally done."

"*Merci.*" Victorine frowned as she turned. "Papa says too much learning isn't healthy for female brains."

"Then why don't you explain that Madame expects us to use our brains like real people? Papa would likely fetch you home. He probably gave more note to Madame's distinguished family background than to her teaching philosophy. I know my father certainly did."

The tinkle of a small bell interrupted Victorine's answer.

"We're not supposed to have lessons today." Elizabeth protested, but just the same, she and Victorine hurried to the end of the hall and down the stairs.

Madame Corday was waiting in the big schoolroom with its large tables and sturdy chairs. Elizabeth and Victorine found Rosamund waiting at their usual table, with younger girls in the row behind them. Elizabeth hastened to take her seat, pushing her wide hoop skirt into place as she sat down.

Madame Corday was an impressive woman, Elizabeth thought, gazing at her teacher. She was still remarkably handsome, even though she was quite old, past thirty at least. Her brown hair was pulled back into a simple French knot, and her wide forehead was pale and still smooth. Her daytime costume was a gown of watered silk, and she looked as elegant as always.

"Is everyone here?" Madame looked over the room. Some of the local girls had already gone home for Christmas, although most would return for the ball, Elizabeth assumed. Who would pass up the opportunity for a dance?

"We're not having lessons today," Madame Corday told the girls. "But you haven't forgotten your weekly letters home?"

Someone in the back groaned, but Madame ignored the interruption.

"But I have to tie rags into my hair to curl it for tonight," Sarah, one of the younger students protested. "And there's a tear in my best stockings that needs to be mended."

"All in good time," Madame said firmly. "Letters first, then you may go."

Elizabeth sighed. Who wanted to write home? Maybe some, or most, of the girls had loving families eager for news. Her own father didn't exactly fit that description. But perhaps her brother John would emerge from his books long enough to read her note. Since she had come to Charleston, he had written her several times, much to her surprise. She had always been in awe of her brother, who was almost a stranger. Ten years her elder, he had been away at school through most of her childhood.

But she might as well get this chore over with. Elizabeth pulled a sheet of good linen paper toward her and dipped her pen into the inkwell.

*Dear Father,*
*My health is good, and my studies are progressing. I hope you and John and everyone*
*on the plantation are well.*

Everyone. . . The memories she always tried to keep at bay sprang into her mind. It was the spring Auntie Mary had fallen ill. Coughing, the slave woman had gone on with her chores, a handkerchief to her flushed face as she bent over the fireplace to stir a bubbling stew. She heated flat irons in the coals to iron William Stafford's fine linen shirts. And as ever, she ruled calmly over the other house servants, giving intelligent direction to the bustle of a busy household.

When six-year-old Elizabeth could escape from her tutor, she'd stayed close to Auntie, receiving hugs instead of scoldings, as well as the first hot corn cake off the griddle and the biggest apple turnover to share with Hannah. Hannah, Mary's daughter, was Elizabeth's maid servant and best friend. The girls were very close in age and had spent their childhoods together. Since her father usually ignored her, they could spend their time more like sisters than servant and mistress.

Later, Mary, her cough wracking her whole body, became too weak to work. She sat by the fire, huddled inside a blanket and sipping herb tea. Elizabeth was still small enough to curl up beside Mary on one side of the big chair, with Hannah on her other side. Listening to Mary's cough, and seeing her grow frailer, had worried Elizabeth. Finally she'd become so frantic she had braved her father in his study.

"You should call the doctor, sir," she'd pleaded. "For Auntie Mary."

"The doctor, for a female slave past her prime? You must learn the economics of plantation life, Elizabeth." Her father frowned.

"But she's really ill," Elizabeth protested. "She could die!"

She thought of the grave in the family cemetery where her own mother lay, the mother she had no memory of. Caroline Stafford had died shortly after Elizabeth's birth. It was Auntie Mary who had nursed her, saved her life, treated her as tenderly as her own small daughter, Hannah, who would become Elizabeth's constant companion. If Auntie Mary died, too, what would they do?

"Please, sir? If not for Auntie Mary, for me?"

"Elizabeth, don't fret so. You are too sentimental." Her father's attention had already returned to the pile of papers in front of him.

The day that Auntie Mary died, her father was out with his horse and guns, shooting a fox that had been raiding the henhouses. There was no one to turn to when Mary coughed a terrible gasping fight for breath, sighed and shut her eyes for the last time.

Clinging to her mother's hand, Hannah had shrieked, then sobbed in anguish.

For Elizabeth, the loss for almost too deep for tears. Although she felt wetness on her cheeks, it brought no relief. She had begged her father for help, and he hadn't listened. All he could see was the monetary worth of a slave. Now Elizabeth had lost the last adult who had truly cared for her.

She hugged Hannah with all her strength.

"Mama, mama," Hannah cried, her eyes already swollen. "What will I do? I've lost my mama."

"I know," Elizabeth whispered. "I'm here."

Mary was buried at the edge of the Stafford plantation, next to other slave graves. Elizabeth had held Hannah's hand and promised herself that she would look after the orphaned slave girl. Whom else did each of them have? Her brother John was away at school, and her father seldom noticed her.

Only once, years later, did William Stafford seem to find something to admire in his only daughter. Her memory of that scene was still vivid, as well. Elizabeth remembered her feelings of terror and delight as she had clung to the back of her father's fiercest stallion, the coarse mane gripped tightly between her fingers as the horse plunged and snorted.

"Get off this minute!" Her tutor, Miss Vaughan, had shrieked. "You'll kill yourself, child. It's not my fault, sir. I left her in the nursery sewing on her sampler." The poor woman had wrung her hands, probably expecting a sharp reprimand from her employer.

But William Stafford had laughed, obviously delighted at he his daughter's display of courage, foolhardy though it might be. "More than her brother's ever done," he noted sardonically. "Hiding behind his books forever and a day, even before he was injured. At least one of my children has some spunk."

Just then, the stallion, too strong for Elizabeth's small hands to control, had tossed its head and reared, dumping her onto the stable yard. The breath knocked out of her, Elizabeth couldn't speak. Her whole body had throbbed from its impact with the hard-packed ground; her hands were stiff from her desperate grip. Tasting gritty dirt and blood–she had bitten her tongue–she heard her father laugh again.

"She's torn her petticoats," Miss Vaughan complained, running to help her up. "She could be lamed for life, just like her brother."

As Elizabeth got slowly to her feet, her father shook his head. "No bones broken, I'd say. I'll get her a horse to ride that's more her size. But no lazy mare, an animal with spirit."

So Elizabeth had been given Smoke, a neat-footed gray gelding, the first tangible sign of her father's affection, and so doubly loved. Sometimes she coaxed Hannah to come along on the placid mare that had been Elizabeth's first mount. What fun they had had, riding together under the shady trees along the river. She and Hannah had never been apart until Elizabeth was sent to Madame Corday's Academy.

*Oh, Hannah, I miss you.* Elizabeth stabbed her pen into the paper until she poked a hole through the heavy sheet.

She had never planned to go away to school. But her father, who had at first encouraged her riding and jumping and shooting, had suddenly decided that his daughter needed a more ladylike polish.

"Jumping your horse through the Byrds' rose garden? Is that any way to go on?" he'd demanded.

"I wasn't really in the garden," Elizabeth tried to argue. "It was just the outer hedge. And
    their governess is the worst prude in—"
But he wouldn't listen.

"Who's going to marry a wild gypsy?" he had retorted, beginning his search for a suitable school.

Startled, Elizabeth forgot to protest. She knew that girls did marry at sixteen or seventeen, but she hadn't yet thought of the possibility of romance. Her father would be thinking of a suitor with a plantation that might rival their own, she told herself woefully. He wouldn't consider that love might be involved.

But despite her misgivings, Elizabeth as usual had no say in the matter. She'd ended up in Charleston, to learn how to be a lady, and without Hannah by her side.

"But Hannah has always been with me," Elizabeth had protested. "How can I leave her behind."

"A slave girl at school—whatever for? You'll need no personal maid, it says so in Madame Corday's letter." Her father had snorted in disdain. "You know it's illegal to teach a slave to read and write. Might as well invite anarchy and rebellion."

Elizabeth for once had bitten back her impetuous words. During all the years when Hannah had sat quietly in the back of the room during Elizabeth's lessons, it didn't seem to occur to anyone else that Hannah, sewing quietly on her mending, had been learning as much, perhaps more, than Elizabeth. It was Hannah who helped Elizabeth later when her mind had wandered during dry lectures, reminded her who had founded Rome or how to do her sums.

And now Hannah was to be left behind, unprotected? Elizabeth wouldn't have it. Storming at her father would do no good; she'd tried that tactic often enough. Later while Elizabeth stalked back and forth in her bed chamber, her too-long-strides caught her dress hem, ripping the trim. Looking at the loose fabric, she'd had an idea. After talking to Hannah, and to her brother, John had added details.

"You're right," he'd said. "You should have her near you. And Hannah's too intelligent to stay and be wasted here."

A little surprised at his comment, but encouraged, nonetheless, Elizabeth faced her father again.

"We could send Hannah to Charleston to learn a trade," she'd said. "That would add greatly to her value, wouldn't it? You have promised to let her go with me when I marry. And she's wonderful with her needle. Look at this trim on my skirt. She could become a dressmaker of unusual ability."

William Stafford gave his daughter a rare smile. "I do believe you're finally learning how the world works, Elizabeth. Practicality, not sentiment. That is an idea to consider."

John, who had college friends in Charleston, had suggested an employer for the slave girl, and the deal was soon made. So Hannah could at least come to the city with her, and now resided several streets over, busy with her own work. Elizabeth saw her only once a week or so, and she missed talking to her every day, but it was better than leaving her friend in Virginia.

Sighing, she added another line to her letter.

*I hope the holidays are merry. Give John my best regards and thank him for the new*
*gloves he sent in my Christmas package. And thank you, sir, for the lengths of fabric for*
*my new gown. It will make a fine show at the Christmas ball.*
*Yours respectfully,          Elizabeth*

There, it was done. Elizabeth glanced down the table at the other girls. Dark-eyed Victorine scribbled busily. She had more reason to write a long letter, Elizabeth thought with a pang of envy. She had heard her friend speak often enough of her doting father, who so pampered his only remaining chld.

And then there was pretty, fair-haired Rosamund, writing carefully in her small, neat script. Though her family wasn't as rich as the families of the other two girls, the Brigham family farm was prosperous. But there was trouble at home, a father bedridden for years, Elizabeth remembered. Perhaps accounted for the momentary withdrawal she sometimes sensed in her normally good-natured friend when, without warning, Rosamund's blue eyes darkened. Or was there something else?

Still, both Rosamund and Victorine had families who cared about them. Elizabeth felt the old emptiness echo inside her. Despite all the suitors who already flocked around her, Elizabeth had found no one special, no one to ease the dark well of loneliness left by her barren childhood. Stephan was charming and good-looking but too easily swayed by her smile. She wanted something more.

## Chapter Two

Elizabeth pushed her letter aside. She felt restless and confined. Sunshine glinted through the tall schoolroom windows. She wished she could wander through town, free and untrammeled. But leaving the school grounds alone required special permission from Madame Corday.

At least there was the ball tonight–she could release some of her restlessness in a fast Virginia reel. But that was hours away. She needed to get out now, to stride through the streets. She wanted to see Hannah, too.

She walked though the big house, finding Madame at last in the ballroom in the west wing with two of the house servants. Fanny was polishing silver, James, perched on a ladder, was carefully cleaning the large crystal chandelier that hung from the ceiling.

Wearing an apron to protect her dress, Madame Corday rubbed a clean cloth over the glas globe from a gaslight. "You must remember not to leave fingerprints, James," she said.

"Madame?" Elizabeth asked.

The schoolmistress looked up, her eyebrows raised. "Finished with your letter home already?"

Elizabeth nodded. "I thought perhaps you might need an errand run. You have so much to do for the party tonight."

Madame smiled knowingly, as if she sensed Elizabeth's urge to get out of the house. "That's very thoughtful, Elizabeth. But James went to the market early for cream and butter and the fresh sea turtle."

Elizabeth knew her shoulders drooped in disappointment.

"On the other hand, my supply of thread is low, and there's sure to be last-minute repairs needed when the girls dress for tonight. Do you know the haberdashery on Market Street that I frequent?"

"Oh, yes, Madame."

"Be sure to put on a shawl," Madame warned. "I know the sun is shining, but the air feels cool. I don't want you to take a chill."

"Yes, Madame," Elizabeth promised. She ran up the stairs, then stopped to catch her breath as her whalebone stays cut into her ribs. In her bed chamber she snatched a shawl from her chest and picked up a small sweet-grass basket. Tossing the shawl around her shoulders, Elizabeth went down the spiral staircase at a more ladylike pace.

Outside, she hurried down the short walk, through the iron gates, and into the street. Skipping a little over the cobblestones, Elizabeth drew a deep breath, or as deep as her tightly drawn corset allowed. The breeze carried a tinge of salt from the harbor, only a few blocks away. Overhead, a seagull floated effortlessly. She paused and threw back her head, relishing her momentary freedom. This was better than lessons and letter-writing! Then she smiled at her thoughts—would she prefer to be one of the vegetable women she passed, who hawked a basket of carrots and turnips?

Of course not, she was a Stafford of Virginia, and she carried a strong pride in her heritage. Indeed, Elizabeth's life would take a predictable course: marriage, husband and children to look after, a plantation house to manage and perhaps parties for amusement. Why did it sound so bleak? She had money and position—she should be thankful for her blessings, as her father often told her.

Trying to cheer herself, she began to walk again, humming to herself. The sun shone, it was almost Christmas, and tonight there was a ball. And she was free to walk rapidly through the streets, the fresh breeze against her face. Her spirits lifted, and she threw back her shawl, enjoying the cool air against her cheeks.

Madame's errand was easily done. With a packet of thread in her basket, Elizabeth hurried on.

She walked past the bustle of the Market, where carcasses of beef and pork, as well as poultry and wild game hung for sale. Bottles of port and other wines lay in dusty stacks. Spoiled meat and other refuse were thrown into the street.

Elizabeth pulled a corner of her shawl over her nose to block the smell and stepped quickly across the intersection. Farther down, she passed the elegant pink facade of Mills Hotel.

On Broad Street, she looked up to see a large banner stretching across the way. It proclaimed, The South Alone Shall Govern The South. Elizabeth didn't fully understand the arguments embroiling the Northern and Southern sections of the country, yet the sign made her pause. Of couse she loved her state, and yet–

"It's not just slavery, although that's a very important issue, both moral and economic," Madame Corday had tried to explain to the class. "Does slavery's economic importance justify its moral ambivalence?"

"The South is mostly farmland, and the North has more industry. The two have different views about tariffs and foreign affairs. And then there's the question of states' rights. Who is the final authority–the federal/national government or the states?"

"Are you saying that slavery is wrong?" one of the students had demanded. "You're not one of those Northern abolitionists, are you, Madame? My father says they're Devil's spawn!"

The schoolroom had felt suddenly tense, and Elizabeth had held her breath, waiting for her schoolmistress's answer.

"There are those in both North and South who feel that slavery is an immoral institution," Madame had answered calmly. "And yes, my husband and I agreed long before his death that we personally would never own another human being." Ignoring the hum of surprise and disapproval from many of the students, Madame had gone on with her lecture.

Startled by her headmistress's personal revelation, Elizabeth had begun to see that the question of slavery versus abolition could be more than just angry editorials in the newspaper. The very next morning, two students who had lived at home and attended classes during the day had been pulled out of school by parents incensed by Madame's comments.

Shaking her head at the memory, Elizabeth reached the dressmaker's shop and found the modiste, Madame Dupris, busy with a customer. The two ladies had their heads bent over a sample of violet silk.

Smiling, Elizabeth, who was a frequent visitor, nodded politely toward the dressmaker and continued on into the back room. She found Hannah beside the window, where the slave girl could catch the best light, her fingers busy with her needle.

"Miss Elizabeth!" Hannah jumped up, dropping her sewing into a basket beside her. Elizabeth squeezed her friend's outstretched hand.

"Look, I've something to show you. The new sewing machine's just arrived, all the way from Philadelphia." Hannah drew her to the side of the room to see a machine with a foot-operated iron treadle below and a stubby black iron top with wheels and cords above. "Isn't it exciting?"

Elizabeth, who hated sewing, had heard of these contraptions, but had never inspected one up close before. "A machine to do the stitching. Whatever is next?"

Hannah laughed. "I have to help it. Look, I sit on the bench like so and push up and down with my foot—a steady rhythm is most important. The thread goes through here, and you guilde the material under the needle. It makes tiny, even stitches, and so quickly—it will save us hours of work and my back won't ache half as much."

"But I bet it can't sew as well as you," Elizabeth insisted loyally.

Hannah's smile lit up her pretty oval face. "Maybe not the fancy stitches. But for plain work, it's really a marvel."

"Does Madame Dupris treat you well, still?" Elizabeth asked, anxiously. "Are you glad you came to Charleston?"

Hannah nodded. "I like it here. I've learned so much. The city is interesting, too, not much like the quiet of the country."

Hannah's smile was contagious. Elizabeth felt her own anxiety fade. "I'm glad."

Just then, Madame Durpris looked in from the front. "Have you finished that flounce, Hannah?"

"I just need one more line of stitches, Madame Dupris," Hannah said swiftly.

The modiste withdrew, but Elizabeth shook her head. "I think that's a hint. I must go."

"Thank you for coming, Miss Elizabeth."

"It was good to see you, Hannah," Elizabeth answered softly. "I miss you."

Hannah smiled as they clasped hands for a moment. Elizabeth felt Hannah's strength. The slave girl had hardy, capable hands. Elizabeth remembered John's remark, years ago. He had just returned from his Northern college, and he spoke for her ears only. "Should a person be less valued because her skin is dark? Is she less human because she is a different color?"

Radical comments for a Virginian. The words had lingered in Elizabeth's mind. Sometimes in the darkness when she should have been sleeping, she had wondered why she slept on a feather bed in a silk nightgown when Hannah lay on a straw pallet. Could it have been the other way around, except for the accident of birth and paler skin?

Slavery was a puzzle Elizabeth had struggled with since childhood, since the first time she'd had to leave Hannah behind.

Invited go a neighboring plantation for another child's birthday party, she'd been incensed to find that Hannah couldn't go, too.

"But there will be cake and lemonade," she'd argued with her father. "Games and songs. It's not fair."

William Stafford had only grunted in derision and lifted her into the carriage. She'd been driven off, haunted by the picture of young Hannah standing disconsolate and lonely back at the plantation. Life was not fair. Young Elizabeth had glimpsed this lesson early. Hannah must know it even better. With an effort Elizabeth pulled her thoughts back to the present. Hannah was watching, her expression quizzical.

"I'll be back before Christmas," Elizabeth promised. "I have a small package for you."

"And I have something for you." Hannah's smile was mischievous. She dipped deep into her sewing basket and withdrew a small bit of lace and ribbon. "It's for your hair."

"It's lovely." Elizabeth examined the finely wrought bow with delight. "I'll wear it tonight. Thank you, Hannah."

As Elizabeth walked out onto the street again, she heard shouting. What was that? A fire, perhaps? Curious, she headed toward the main street and saw groups of men talking with great animation. What was going on? She strolled around several groups of excited citizens, unable to catch anyone's eye.

"St. Andrew's Hall," a tall man was saying. "But it's only a voice vote. It will have to be done again, in legal fashion."

"Legal," a short, balding gentleman objected. "What's legal about secession?"

"Man, have you no wits at all?" someone else shouted angrily. "Would you have those Yankees telling us how to run our own state? Our own homes?"

"But the Constitution—"

"What about the rights of the states? Didn't the Constitution guarantee that?" the tall man shouted, gesturing widely with his hands. His right arm grazed Elizabeth's shoulder, and he twisted to get a look at her.

"Here, young lady. You'd best get yourself home."

"But what is it?" Elizabeth demanded, determined to know the source of all the agitation.

"It's the state convention," another man told her. "We have to show those Northern states they can't dictate to us!"

"And that rascal Lincoln!" someone added. "Didn't he say himself, before he was elected, 'This government cannot endure, permanently half slave and half free'?"

"They can't tell us how to live—or whether we can keep our slaves," another man put in, his face flushed. "Why, how would we run our plantations? They'd miss our cotton and rice soon enough!"

Still confused, Elizabeth turned away. She remembering Madame Corday mentioning the state convention, but Elizabeth had paid little attention. When she passed the office of a local newspaper, the *Charleston Mercury*, she saw leaflets being tossed from an upper window. She joined the crowd on the street who were snatching for a sheet. When she had captured a handbill, she backed away, trying to find room to read it.

Around her, men shouted and threw up their hats. Boys ran up and down the street, waving their caps; some had small flags.

Holding the paper tightly, Elizabeth read, *THE UNION IS DISSOLVED*!

## Chapter Three

Elizabeth hurried back to the Academy. Shouts still echoed behind her. What did it mean, this talk of secession?

She found Madame Corday in the kitchen, checking on the turtle soup that bubbled on the hearth.

"I have the thread, Madame," Elizabeth set the basket down– "and this." She held out the wrinkled handbill she had collected on the street. Madame put down a wooden spoon to glance at the paper.

Elizabeth's heart beat faster when she saw the headmistress's face pale. "What does it signify?" she asked, her voice quiet amid the busy hustle of the kitchen.

"If South Carolina really secedes–the state has threatened to do so before–that means it is leaving the Union, leaving the United States," Madame told her.

"You mean the United States will break into pieces? Can that happen?"

"The state convention believes that it can," Madame Corday said. She sighed and closed her eyes for a moment as if to shut out some unwelcome vision. "You'd better go in. We'll have dinner very soon, and then you'll want to change."

Elizabeth found most of the girls already collected in the dining room.

"Where have you been?" Rosamund looked up from her usual seat as Elizabeth slipped into the next chair.

"Running errands. I heard—" Elizabeth bit off her words as Madame entered the room and took her place at the head of the table. They all lowered their heads for grace, then Fanny entered with a large tureen and ladled out thick soup.

"What did you hear while you were out?" Rosamund asked, dipping a round spoon into her rose-sprigged china soup bowl.

"Nothing, it doesn't matter." Elizabeth didn't want to think about the handbill, about secession and arguments in the street. She could tell Rosamund later, after the Christmas ball.

When dinner had ended, the two floors upstairs were full of activity as twenty-two young ladies brought out all their finery. Elizabeth caught a glimpse of Sarah in the hall, her hair still tied in rag strips, her face smeared with a mixture of oatmeal, lemon juice, and honey.

"It lightens the skin," the younger girl explained earnestly.

"Stay away from a bee hive," another girl quipped. Some of the other students giggled. Sarah flushed and hurried back to her own room.

"That wasn't kind," Rosamund admonished the younger girls, and they scattered, hastening back to their rooms. Lowering her voice, Rosamund added to Elizabeth, "Sarah worries about her freckles, but they really aren't that bad. Now, help me tighten my stays, please."

Elizabeth crossed the room and tugged hard on the corset strings while Rosamund clung to her bedpost, panting a little.

"Oh, oh." Rosamund gasped for breath. "One thing about living on a farm. You can't wear stays and hoe a corn field. Enough, that's all I can stand."

They changed places.

It was Elizabeth's turn to shed her day dress and gasp while Rosamund tightened her friend's corset strings. Then Elizabeth adjusted her hoops and fitted the wide skirt of the green ball gown over them. Next she slipped into the satin bodice, its deep neckline trimmed in white ruffles. "Confound these buttons!"

Rosamund put down her own satin skirt and hurried to help. When the buttons were done, Elizabeth spend a few minutes working on her hair, then picked up the bow that Hannah had given her and positioned it carefully in her glossy chestnut waves. She had pulled her hair up and back, but a few curls escaped to frame her face. She peeked into the looking glass. Not bad, she thought. Stephen should forget his sulkiness when he saw the picture she made in her new ballgown.

She turned and saw Rosamund adjusting her own bodice, trimmed in simple crocheted lace.

"The color suits you. It brings out the blue in your eyes," Elizabeth told her.

"Thank you. We cut it down to fit me. It was my mother's dress when she was younger. It's not as grand as your dress or Victorine's."

Elizabeth knew that Rosamund was conscious of the fact that she had much less spending money than many of the girls at school, including Victorine and Elizabeth herself. She also had fewer and less elegant clothes.

"No one will be as grand as *la petite Victorine*. We'll simply have to be handmaidens at Her Majesty's court."

Rosamund laughed quietly at the remark, and Elizabeth was pleased to have lightened her friend's mood. The ball would be a big success, she just knew it. And she could dance and laugh and forget about politics and danger altogether.

"Coming, Victorine?" she called into the bedroom across the hall. "We're going down."

"So early?" Victorine glance out of her doorway. Her black hair was drawn up in an elaborate coiffure topped with a tulle flounce with lappets of tulle and lace. Diamond eardrops glistened in her ears, and strands of large pearls looped her neck. The pink satin dress with an overlay of Brussels lace gave her the delicate look of a storybook princess. Excitement made her dark eyes gleam. "I want to make a grand entrance after all the guest have arrived, just like my *maman* used to do. Why waste the effect, *n'est pas*?"

"If you like," Elizabeth told her. "But I don't want to wait. I want to see the chandeliers all lit up, and the bowls of fruit and greenery that Madame arranged to adorn the tables. And the food–Madame has ices and meringues and three types of cakes!"

"Come, Elizabeth," Rosamund said. "I'll come down with you."

They both slowly descended the wide spiral staircase. When they reached the ground floor, Elizabeth paused to glance out the tall windows. She could hear the clatter of horses' hooves on the cobblestones and the creak of carriages and buggies as their passengers climbed down to the wide stepping-stone.

From the ballroom in the west wing, she heard a violin being tuned. As she turned, she felt Rosamund touch her arm.

"I'm so excited," Rosamund's usually calm voice wavered. "But I'm frightened, too. This isn't a quilting bee or a barn raising. I'm not from a big plantation like most of y'all, Elizabeth. What if I do something dreadful? Forget the steps to a dance? Drop my fork or spill a glass of champagne?"

"Don't be foolish." Elizabeth gave Rosamund's gloved hand a quick squeeze. "When Madame gave us dancing lessons in the ballroom, you did as well as anyone."

"But the chandeliers were draped in dust-cloths, then, and there was no one to see me but the other girls. This is different."

"You will not make a spectacle of yourself, Rosamund. You have more sense than anyone else I know, now use it. If you're nervous, you watch me and do what I do," Elizabeth said, her tone firm. "No, watch Victorine. She never does *anything* wrong."

Rosamund giggled.

Elizabeth picked up her skirts and glided carefully down the hall. "Come along."

They entered through the double doors. The ballroom was a sight to make anyone's heart beat faster. Against the silver-striped wallpaper, gas lights blazed brightly. The crystal chandeliers made a splendid display, and the polished hardwood floor glittered with reflected light. Wax candles in silver candelabra pinpointed small tables against the far wall.

# HEARTS DIVIDED
27

Seductive aromas of spicy food from the adjacent dining room mixed with the slight odor of the gaslights and the fragrances of the guests' heavy perfumes. The small group of hired musicians at the back of the ballroom produced a lilting Mendelssohn melody, which was punctuated by bursts of laughter and conversation.

The guests themselves added to the kaleidoscope of color and motion. Bright gowns and glittering jewels embellished the women, while dark evening suits and pomaded hair made the gentlemen look suitably elegant.

Elizabeth drew a breath of pleasure and anticipation.

"Uh, Miss Elizabeth," a male voice quivered. "Do you remember me? We met at the church tea last month. Robert Hansen, at your service. I'm a junior at the College of Charleston. Perhaps you could put me down for a dance?" He smiled timidly at her.

Elizabeth looked the young man up and down. He was short, not quite meeting her at eye level, and stocky, and his hair was carroty red, an unfortunate shade, she thought. Freckles covered his round face.

*He should ask Sarah about her remedy for fading spots*, she thought, swallowing a laugh. "How nice to see you again, Mr. Hanson," she said, her voice smooth. "I'm waiting for

someone and I'm afraid all my dances are spoken for. But have you met my friend, Rosamund Brigham?"

Robert's face fell in obvious disappointment but he brightened as Rosamund smiled at him.

"How do you do?" He bowed deeply over Rosamund's hand, giving her a moment to throw Elizabeth a telling glance. But when he asked, "May I have the honor?" Rosamund allowed him to lead her to the dance floor.

Elizabeth watched them for a moment, until she was assured that Rosamund was gliding as smoothly through the pattern as any of the other dancers. At least her friend wouldn't feel timid dancing with Mr. Hanson, she told herself. Then a more familiar voice caught her ear.

"Miss Elizabeth! There you are. I must say, you look splendid in that gown."

Elizabeth smiled at Stephen's enthusiasm. He looked very fine, himself. His blond hair was combed into careful, pomaded waves, and his dark formal suit and gray silk waistcoat were especially trim, his white cravat artfully tied. He stood tall and straight, and she knew already that he was an accomplished dancer–it would be a grand party.

"I'm so glad you were well enough to come, sir," she murmured sedately, but she flashed him a mischievous smile that made him flush.

"It was a nasty cut," he declared, showing her a tiny bandage on his wrist, just visible past his spotless kid glove. "Bled all over the place and hurt like the devil–oh, sorry. Not that I took note of it, of course."

"Of course," she agreed.

"But I wouldn't have missed the Christmas Ball–and the chance to dance with you. You did promise me the reel, and at least two waltzes."

"Did I, Mr. Hall?" she teased, watching his smile waver.

"Now, Miss Elizabeth," Stephen tugged at his tight collar. "You did say—"

She flipped open her fan and raised it to cover all but a corner of her lips, which curved into a flirtatious smile. "Of course, I did," she agreed. "I should be most disappointed to miss the pleasure of waltzing with you."

Stephen beamed. "I should say I deserve it, after being wounded on your account, so to speak."

Elizabeth's laughter bubbled over. "Such a dreadful wound, too."

Stephen looked offended. "Well, it did hurt. And I did do it for you. I could have gotten into a whale of trouble, Miss Elizabeth, if anyone had seen us."

Elizabeth allowed her smile to fade. "I'm surprised at your lack of spirit, sir. Is this the way the gentlemen of South Carolina display their courage?"

"No, no, I wasn't saying that I minded," he hastened to add. "Really, for you, I'd dare anything."

He reached for her hand, and she could feel the tight grip of his fingers through her gloves.

"May I get you some punch? Or would you like to dance?"

The musicians were striking up again, and she heard the tune with pleasure.

"Dance, of course." She took his arm and they made their way onto the floor. He led her through the dance steps with practiced ease. They danced two in a row, then Elizabeth gave the next tune to a good-looking classmate of Stephen's, before returning to her beau. After the next dance, they paused long enough to stroll into the dining room and attend to the well-filled tables of food.

Elizabeth ate a few bites of peach-flavored ice and meringue topped with candied dried fruit, wishing her tightly laced corset allowed her to indulge a bigger appetite. Stephen filled his plate with oyster gumbo and smoked turkey and then made two forays into the sweets. He swallowed a mouthful of sherry trifle, then muttered, "Madame sets a fine table. Nothing like this at our school, I assure you. Fortunate you're here. Very important, learning to keep a good house. For when you're a married lady, I mean."

"There are more important things than keeping house, Stephen."

His expression polite but puzzled, he gulped another bite. Sighing, Elizabeth put down her plate. This was no time to quarrel. "Hurry," she told him. "They're beginning a new tune. I think it's a waltz."

Stephen gulped down his last bite, grabbed her hand and led her back to the dance floor. As they began, Elizabeth caught a glance of some late arrivals over his shoulder. Surely that wasn't an army uniform?

Then Stephen whirled her, and Elizabeth tried to concentrate on the pleasure of the dance. She was here to have fun, she reminded herself, not to worry about politics. But when the music faded, she risked another look.

The tall young man in the blue uniform heldhimself very straight. He had dark hair and a brooding expression. For an instant, their gazes met. Those dark eyes seemed to cut right through her; she suddenly found it hard to take a breath. Why did she feel as if the whole room had paused, and the world had stopped its spinning?

She had time for only a glance before Stephen turned her around to face him. But the stranger in blue seemed imprinted on her memory, and she was conscious of him even when she had turned her back.

Why was he here? Why had this stranger come out tonight in his dress uniform, when the whole town was in an uproar, angry at everything Northern? Was he so dense as to not be aware of the emotions of Charleston residents? She remembered the arrogance of the banner stretched across Broad Street, the outraged voices of the men in the avenue. Dimly she realized Stephen had spoken.

"We got out of class early," he said. "All the uproar in town— did you hear?"

"Yes." she nodded absently, then glanced up at him with more attention. "You don't think this secession business will amount to anything, do you?"

He looked serious for a moment, then shrugged. "South Carolina planters are angry, Miss Elizabeth. You should her my father on the subject. All the talk up North about Abolition—it's well and good for those Yankee traders and factory owners, but how can we grow our rice and cotton and indigo without slave labor? Abolition would ruin the whole Southern economy. And why should Yankees be allowed to tell us what to do?"

"But do you think slavery is really such a fine thing?" Elizabeth thought uneasily of Hannah, so intelligent and kind-hearted.

"Most people treat their slaves well," Stephen told her. "Why should anyone with sense mistreat a valuable piece of property?"

Elizabeth signed. It was hard to think of Hannah as *property*. "But—" she began.

"Don't worry yourself," Stephen told her, assuming his gallant tone. "We'll take care of this—the menfolk, I mean. No need for you to fret. Never let it be said that Southern gentlemen don't look out for their ladies."

Elizabeth could almost hear an echo of her father's voice, although he never sounded so—so genuinely concerned for her anxiety.

Troubled, she looked away, straight into the blue uniformed stranger's dark eyes. He seemed to watch her intently. Elizabeth repressed a shiver. Excitement prickled her skin and made her breath deeply.

"Why is that fellow staring at you?" Stephen abruptly demanded. "Talk about gall! Showing up at a Charleston party in his Union blue. I've a good mind to call him out myself, just on principle."

"Wait!" Elizabeth put a restraining hand on his arm. "Don't spoil Madame's Christmas Ball. You're a guest, as well. And duels are horrid. I don't want to see you with any more wounds."

"Would you care?" Stephen captured her hand and pressed it tightly, seeming touched by her concern. "Would you really care,

Miss Elizabeth? He moved closer, and she saw how his fine, light lashes rimmed his blue eyes, eyes eager now with anticipation.

"Of course I would." Elizabeth said, but she withdrew her hand from his grip. "I prefer you in one piece. You wouldn't dance nearly as well, otherwise."

She smiled at him over the edge of her fan, and Stephen seemed satisfied, at least for the moment.

Elizabeth stole another glance at the Union soldier. He had made his bow to Madame and now stood talking to Rosamund. He was about twenty, perhaps, she guessed. And he had a fine pair of shoulders.

"My parents were pleased to meet you at last month's church tea," Stephen was saying. "My sisters said you were dreadfully pretty. And from a fine family, my father noted. He met your father, you know, on a trip to Richmond last year."

Elizabeth nodded. She could think of nothing but the stranger in uniform. What was he saying to Rosamund? She interrupted Stephen.

"I do feel for my friend Rosamund. She doesn't know many gentlemen in Charleston. First she endured two dances with that boring Mr. Hanson, and now she's stuck at the side of the room with the elderly ladies. Why don't you give her the pleasure of a dance with a really accomplished partner?"

Stephen smiled. "I'd rather dance with you, but if you wish it, of course. You're very kind-hearted, Elizabeth."

Elizabeth felt a twinge of guilt, but she ignored it as they made their way across the ballroom, stepping in front of Rosamund and the Union soldier.

"Miss Brigham, you remember Mr. Hall," Elizabeth said formally. "He was hoping for the pleasure of a dance."

"How kind," Rosamund murmured. "Miss Stafford, Mr. Hall, Lieutenant Adam Cranfield, lately of West Point." The gentlemen exchanged slight bows, then Rosamund accepted

Stephen's arm with apparent pleasure and walked beside him toward the dance floor.

At last Elizabeth could take a good look at this bold stranger. He was tall, at least six feet, she calculated. His eyes were a dark brown, his brows heavy, his expression contained. Suddenly her stomach felt hollow and her mouth dry. She had the strange notion that they were all alone in their own time and space while the music and chatter and bustle of the room receded. She could hear only his deep, pleasing voice, see only the searching eyes, firm lips and strong chin.

"A pleasure, Miss Stafford," the young officer said. He gave her a correct but slightly stiff bow, and she slipped into a demure curtsey. "It was kind of Madame Corday to invite me to share your holiday celebration." His accent was clipped; it sounded hard to her Southern ears.

"So far from home at Christmas. Are you visiting in Charleston?" Elizabeth brought her fan into play, hoping he would notice her well-shaped eyes.

But he glanced at her only briefly, then turned his gaze to the dance floor. He had been staring at her long enough from across the room, why did he ignore her now? He didn't seem to know much about flirting–boorish, these Yankees, she told herself.

Her judgment was harsh, she knew. After all, her dear cousin Lucy had married a Northerner and now lived in Washington City. Still–

"I'm stationed at Fort Moultrie, ma'am."

"How exciting for you," Elizabeth said. She began to feel miffed. He made her heart beat faster, just by the merest glance, but now he looked away. Was he watching Rosamund, whirling across the floor with Stephen? Did her own charms have no effect on this unpolished young man? And why did this thought bother her so much?"

He seemed to note the wryness of her tone, because he turned back to look at her. "I suppose it might become so."

His tone was serious, and she didn't want to talk politics, not tonight.

"Would you care to join them?" she asked tartly when his gaze wandered again.

He shrugged. "I'm afraid I'm not very accomplished on the dance floor."

Really, he was too infuriating.

"I am," Elizabeth said. She tucked her hand though his arm and moved forward. Looking startled, the young lieutenant accompanied her out onto the polished hardwood floor.

"Are you planning to lead?" he asked, raising those satyr-like dark brows.

"If necessary, but I think you'll pass muster," Elizabeth said. "You look reasonably intelligent."

"I'll try not to disappoint you," Lieutenant Cranfield replied.

He gripped her hand and placed his other carefully at her waist to guide her though the dance. They moved with the rhythm of the flowing music. He danced competently enough, despite his disparaging words, though not with Stephen's easy grace.

But he held her tightly, guided her firmly across the floor as they turned and swayed. Elizabeth felt almost dizzy, but not from the whirling to the music, not from the excitement of the party. This tall stranger affected her as Stephen, with his boyish enthusiasm, never had.

For a moment it all blurred together–the light from the sparkling chandeliers above them, the moving patterns of the other dancers in colorful gowns and dark suits, the lilting notes of the music. She was aware most of how firmly he held her hand, of his almost intimate touch on her waist, of the thick dark lashes that shaded his eyes, and of the faint scar on his chin. She was breathing too quickly. Elizabeth forced herself to look away.

She was not the kind of girl to fall for a good-looking face, Elizabeth scolded herself. Not that he was handsome in the usual way, exactly. But for all his apparent reserve, there was something in the depths of his eyes that made her want to take his hand, touch his cheek. When he looked down at her, she sensed a fierceness behind the mask, strong feelings held barely in check. He gripped her hand even more tightly.

The music around them, the waltz would end too soon. Elizabeth wished that it would never stop, that Adam Cranfield would never release her. She felt at home in his arms.

The tall Yankee did not seem disposed to conversation, so Elizabeth spoke up. "So silent. Are you minding your steps?"

Her tone was more tart than she'd intended, but the turmoil inside her was unnerving. This had never happened to her before. She was used to being the one in control, leading eager young men through flirtatious dances—and not just on the ballroom floor.

He looked into her eyes, and his mouth turned up into an almost grin. "A bit, yes. Do you always say whatever you please?"

"I'm afraid so," Elizabeth said, with no pretense of regret. "It makes me a difficult person to know."

"I'd already decided that," he agreed.

Elizabeth bit her lip, looking away. She didn't know whether to fire back a quick retort or to laugh. *He is supposed to protest and add a compliment or two*, she thought. *This is not the way the game is played. Has no one ever taught this Northerner how to flirt? Are the girls so dull and proper where he comes from?*

Then she had an even more lowering thought. *Does he prefer Rosamund? Rosamund, who is polite and soft-spoken, with the flash of quick intelligence beneath the surface?* This notion was too painful to pursue. Again Elizabeth spoke quickly, her tone almost rude. "I supposed you're not familiar with Southern women?"

"On the contrary," the young officer replied, his voice cool. "My mother was from Virginia. You remind me of her."

His tone made the comment almost an insult. Elizabeth drew a breath, trying to frame an answer. What was wrong with women from Virginia?

The waltz music faded, and the dancers around them halted, bowing and laughing. Elizabeth paused, still curiously reluctant to step out of his grip. She looked up to meet his dark eyes. What emotion glittered in those smoky depths? And what had he meant by that double-edged comment?

"Thank you for the dance," Lieutenant Cranfield told her, his tone grave. "If I need more instruction, I shall return to your tutelage."

Lifting her chin, Elizabeth stepped back. "I think you need instruction in polite conversation!"

"No doubt."

He appeared unshaken by her retort, and Elizabeth felt somehow bested. She tried to smile politely, to show him she was unfazed, but her lips felt stiff. His words had stung.

She mustn't allow anyone else to see her so distracted. Elizabeth the flirt had met her match. This man would not jump to her every whim. Elizabeth turned abruptly and hurried into the almost empty dining room. Passing a side table, she pretended to consider the ravaged plates of pastry and tried to calm herself.

A touch on her shoulder made her jump. She looked around. Adam Cranfield stood very close. She could see a vein in his temple throb. His dark eyes were like velvet.

"Did I upset you? I'm sorry. I find it hard to remember all the polite nothings, especially with you."

"Why with me?" Elizabeth whispered.

"Because you're too real for empty phrases." His tone was low, even intimate.

Elizabeth felt her mouth go dry. She didn't know how to answer. Perhaps frivolous words would never satisfy her again, either.

He moved even closer. Elizabeth looked up into his eyes. Just then, outside the windows, a brilliant flash of light rose upward against the night sky, and a sharp, sizzling sound shattered the night.

## Chapter Four

'What is it?" Elizabeth demanded, clutching Lieutenant Cranfield's arm.

"Someone shot off a rocket." His expression had altered–the moment was lost. Abashed, Elizabeth dropped her hand.

Now a great wave of shouting beat against the windowpanes. Past the open gates, Elizabeth saw a crowd of men in the streets, yelling, cheering, some bearing torches, others waving flags. All around, she heard the deep sound of church bells tolling.

The ball guests, as if with one thought, moved toward the hallway and on through the outer doors and down the steps into the damp, chill garden. Adam Cranfield pushed his way through the crowd. Elizabeth tried to follow, but she soon lost sight of him. More disappointed than she would allow herself to show, Elizabeth looked toward the street.

"It's done," a man shouted. "The Ordinance of Secession is signed. South Carolina is an independent commonwealth!"

Cheers and more shouts followed. Elizabeth drew a deep breath. It had happened, then. Secession was more than a word, much more than a threat.

Rosamund moved up beside her, her face pale in the light reflected from the house. "It sounds very lonely, doesn't it?" she shouted so that Elizabeth could hear. "Just South Carolina, all by itself."

Elizabeth nodded.

But Stephen Hall had come up beside them. He had heard her words, as well. "It won't be just South Carolina for long, you'll see!" he yelled back. "The rest of the South will follow. We'll show those Yankees just how little we care for their bullying."

Madame Corday had said the South had talked of secession for years, Elizabeth remembered. But few people expected an actual war. Still–

"It won't mean fighting, will it?" Elizabeth stared at Stephen's wide grin.

"War?" His face lit up even more. "I should wish, but no such luck. The Yankees will never risk their precious necks just to keep us in the Union. They have no stomach for it, wait and see. But a war would be grand."

At the mention of Yankees, Elizabeth couldn't help looking around once more for Lieutenant Cranfield, one of those Northerners whose courage Stephen was impugning so easily. Was that his tall form standing back by the door, just visible over the heads of other party guests? She wasn't sure. She longed to hear what else he might have said to her if they had not been interrupted.

Elizabeth bit her lip, and she saw her own concern mirrored in Rosamund's face. They were standing now by the edge of the open gates, fighting not to be pushed even farther into the street.

Then some of the crowd passed on, and a loosely grouped band marched through the avenue. They were playing with more enthusiasm than skill.

Victorine pushed her way through the party-goers to stand with her friends. She clutched a shawl closely around her shoulders. "*Idiots*," she said, nodding toward the confusion. "They've ruined our party."

Elizabeth could share her friend's chagrin, especially when she saw many of the male guests joining the throng, moving away with the masses of people in the street.

"Mr Hall!" She turned in time to see him edge away. "Where are you going?"

"My apologies to Madame Corday, and to you," he told her quickly, bending over her hand. "But this is history, Miss Elizabeth! Someday we'll tell our grandchildren about this glorious evening."

"Glorious, indeed," she muttered, watching force his way into the mob.

"We'd better get in or Madame will scold," Rosamund said. "This crowd could get wild."

For once, Elizabeth agreed with her more cautious friend. "I suppose so. The party's already spoiled. What a fuss men can make."

Turning, she made her way through the remaining guests, ignoring the excited chatter. There was no sign of the young lieutenant. Perhaps he had slipped away quietly. It was no time for a Yankee to be noticed on the streets of Charleston.

This thought merely added to her depression. Her excited anticipation of the ball, her unexpected response to the stranger in the Union uniform–all shattered.

The only people left in the ballroom were elderly ladies, heads together as they peered through the windowpanes. Elizabeth climbed the spiral staircase to her bed chamber. In the silence of her room, she took out the faded journal she had had since she was a child. She found a blank page and scribbled quickly.

*The Christmas ball was grand until the commotion in the street ruined it all.*

*Secession is here. And I met a Yankee who is going to change my life. He*

*    may not know it yet, but I know.*

She was clutching the pencil too hard. Straightening her cramped fingers, Elizabeth drew a deep breath, trying to allow the tension, the excitement, the disappointment to flow out of her. But the memory of Adam Cranfield remained as vivid as ever.

Later, Rosamund joined her, and they both shed their finery, quickly pulling on nightgowns in the chilly air of the bedchamber. Elizabeth looked across the room.

"What did you talk to him about, the Union officer, I mean?"

Rosamund paused, then tied her nightcap beneath her chin. "We discussed *Uncle Tom's Cabin.* He said it's all the rage up north."

"You've read that book? My brother mentioned it, but Father wouldn't allow it in our house. Stephen Hill says it's full of lies about the South."

"Perhaps. It's an affecting story," Rosamund told her. "About an old slave beaten by a villainous owner, a slave girl and her baby fleeing across icy rivers to freedom, chased by dogs and evil slave catchers."

Shuddering, Elizabeth pulled back the covers and scrambled into bed. "We're not like that! As Stephen said, most people take good care of their slaves. Does Lieutenant Cranfield think we are all villains?" She felt her heart beat faster at the thought. Was this why he had spoken so sternly of his Southern mother?

She could barely make out Rosamund's shrug beneath the thick quilts. "I don't know. He's hard to read, this lieutenant."

Elizabeth nodded. "He made me feel—"

She paused, and Rosamund stared at her with obvious curiosity. Elizabeth had almost said, *I will never be the same.* Yet she couldn't admit that a man had affected her so strongly after one meeting, not even to Rosamund.

"Well?"

"That I've done something wrong, but I don't know what," she finished, lamely. "What did you think of him?"

"Very reserved. Intelligent and well educated." Rosamund's tone was thoughtful.

"And?" Elizabeth stared hard at her friend.

Rosamund smiled and blew out the candle beside the bed. "And he has a fine pair of shoulders."

Elizabeth pulled rather too hard at the thick quilt. She thought she heard the other girl laugh softly.

The noise outside went on all night, and once she even heard the thunder of a cannon firing. It was the noise that kept her turning restlessly in her bed, Elizabeth told herself. That and the glare of bonfires in the street. Not a pair of fine shoulders or thick brows lifted in sardonic amusement.

The celebration continued for three days. On the day before Christmas, they were released from their usual lessons. The local girls had already gone home, but a dozen or more students stayed on. Many, like Victorine, were too far from home to make the trip for only a few days. Rosamund's family couldn't afford the extra expense. Elizabeth's father seemed to assume she would stay at school, and she didn't protest.

The afternoon was fair and sunny. In the small sitting room, Elizabeth had dropped her sewing in her lap. Plagued by thoughts of Adam Cranfield, she was too restless for a task she detested. Victorine sewed sedately, while Rosamund read aloud to them from *A Tale of Two Cities*.

Fanny came to the door, her dark eyes dancing. "A visitor for you, Miss Elizabeth."

Elizabeth jumped quickly to her feet, and she heard Victorine giggle.

"Thank you, Fanny. I'll see him in the small waiting room," she told the house servant as calmly as she could.

"How do you know it's a *he*, eh?" Victorine teased, looking up from her embroidery.

Elizabeth made a face at the petite girl, but she composed her expression as she left the room. Anticipation rose inside her. But when she entered the smaller room and found blond hair instead of dark and blue eyes instead of deep brown, she couldn't suppress a flicker of disappointment.

"Your servant, Miss Elizabeth," Stephen Hall rose at once to his feet. "A small token of my esteem in honor of Christmas." His speech sounded rehearsed.

She accepted the box of bonbons, trying not to laugh. "Thank you, sir. This is an unexpected pleasure." Elizabeth gave him her hand to bow over. "Are you out of classes now for the holiday?"

He shrugged the question aside. "Who can concentrate on books at a time like this. I hope you might be free to walk with me. I have something to show you."

"Let me ask Madame Corday," Elizabeth said. She had a package to deliver to Hannah as well, and she was always happy to get a few minutes of freedom.

Fortunately, Madame knew and approved of Stephen, and she gave Elizabeth permission to go out. Once Elizabeth picked up her basket and donned a warm pelisse, they ventured onto the cobblestone streets.

"What did you want to show me?" Elizabeth asked Stephen, who held her arm with eager solicitude.

"Here it is, come inside."

To her mystification, they entered a tailor's shop.

Stephen called merrily to the man at the back. "I'm here again, Mr. Perris. Is it ready?"

"Ah, yes, very close. Another fitting will be required, and then I can put in the finishing touches," the elderly man said. He approached them holding a jacket of gray cloth, which Stephen slipped eagerly into. A young black man held a white sash ready.

"What do you think, Miss Elizabeth? I've joined a militia unit to defend our state if those Yankees decide to make a fuss. Doesn't it look fine?"

He adjust the sash and preened a bit, turning to examine his reflection in the looking glass at the side of the shop. Elizabeth bit her lip to contain a smile.

"You look truly handsome," she said. "But what about college? What will your father say?"

"My father's a true Carolinian. He's proud as Punch. And we'll do our drilling after classes. Shoot, Miss Elizabeth, all the fellows are signing up. What kind of gentleman wouldn't protect his own home?"

The tailor brought out more material draped over his arm, and he and Stephen conferred for a few moments.

"Our trousers will have a stripe down the side," Stephen explained to Elizabeth after the two men had spoken. "And the jacket will have epaulets on the shoulders, of course, and gold braid and brass buttons."

"A fine choice," Mr. Perris hastened to add. "Much better than the Zouaves with their baggy pants or the Highlanders' kilts."

"Kilts?" Elizabeth said. "Are fancy uniforms all you men are thinking of?"

Stephen flushed. "Of course not, but we might as well have some fun. After all, this will be our first taste of military action."

"I thought you said that the Yankees wouldn't fight!" Elizabeth swallowed hard.

"They probably won't, but we have to be prepared," Stephen answered. "If we sit on our hands, the Yankees will think that we're afraid."

"I don't like it." Elizabeth shook her head.

The tailor moved to the back of the shop, muttering measurements beneath his breath.

"Of course you would feel that way. A lady would. But war makes a man out of you," Stephen explained. "It's a fine thing to protect one's state. We've been reading 'The Charge of the Light Brigade.' It does make me wish for a chance to gallop into battle, with th flags flying high and the cannons roaring, my fellow soldiers at my side."

His enthusiasm was contagious. Her fear faded, and Elizabeth felt her own imagination stirred by the picture he painted. For a moment she almost wished she were a man, also, riding off to battle in a bright new uniform, glorious and invincible.

"I'm sure you'll be a credit to you family," she said.

"And to you. Will you be proud of me, too, Elizabeth?" He took her hand and squeezed it, his handsome face eager.

But her heart beat calmly, and her breathing was unhurried. Where was the unexpected thrill that the young West Pointer had elicited the night of the Christmas ball? Why couldn't she feel the same way with Stephen whose blue eyes were filled with hope as he gazed at her?

"I'm sure I'll be proud of you," she answered. "But–but I must run an errand of my own, and then get back to the Academy before dark or Madame will give me a scold."

"Of course," Stephen agreed, released her hand. "I need to finish my fitting. But I'll escort you back when I'm done."

"Thank you, but there's no need," Elizabeth said quickly. "I have permission to go alone. Thank you again for the delicious candy. The new uniform will be most handsome, and the gentleman wearing it very distinguished."

She left him smiling in the small shop as the tailor returned to pin the lengths of wool for his trousers.

The dressmaker's shop where Hannah labored was only a short distance away. Elizabeth went in through the front door, and the black woman seated on the stool looked up quickly.

"It's only me, Maizie," Elizabeth told her, smiling. "Is Hannah here?"

"She's in the back room, Miz Elizabeth." The woman returned her smile, then looked back to the sewing in her lap.

Elizabeth hurried through the inner door and found Hannah in the rear storeroom, standing in front of a dress form.

"Oh, it looks splendid," Elizabeth said. "Is this your own design?" She examined the riding habit with an experienced eye. It was navy blue, with scarlet braid on the shoulders and lapel.

"Miss Elizabeth, yes." Hannah looked justifiably proud of her work. "Some of it, at least. Madame Dupris helped me shape the pattern. But the fancywork is all mine. Do you really like it?"

"It's beautiful," Elizabeth assured her. "You're going to be better than Madame Dupris herself before you're done."

"Hush! Don't say that too loud." Hannah's eyes twinkled.

"Look, I've brought you your Christmas gifts." Elizabeth handed over the basket and watched Hannah lift out its contents, exclaiming with pleasure.

There were two lengths of bright calico, which Elizabeth knew that Hannah would make into pretty dresses for herself, and at the bottom, a thick woolen shawl.

"I knitted it myself at the Academy," Elizabeth told her. "Sone of the stitches may be a bit wobbly–I'll never be as good with a needle as you–but it's warm, at least."

"It's very nicely done and will feel most welcome when winter winds blow off the ocean," Hannah assured her. "And it will be special because you made it."

"Can you come out for a walk?" Elizabeth asked.

Hannah hesitated.

"Just a short one," Elizabeth added. "The afternoon is lovely, and the wind not so cold. Shall I ask permission of Madame Dupris?"

Even though Hannah insisted she was treated well by her employer, Elizabeth worried that she would be kept sewing too long indoors, missing the benefits of fresh air and exercise.

"She's having her afternoon nap." Hannah glanced toward the upper floor. "I don't think she would mind, since it's you. And I've gotten much done since this morning."

"Good," Elizabeth said. "Come, let's not waste more time. We can talk as we walk."

Hannah wrapped her new shawl around her shoulders. She left word with Maizie, and she and Elizabeth stepped outside into the sunlight and brisk winter air.

"The hair bow you made for me was a great success" Elizabeth told her. "I wore it for the Christmas ball, and all the other girls admired it."

Hannah looked gratified. "Do you enjoy the party?"

Elizabeth shrugged. "At first, yes. The ball room was a grand sight, and my new gown was splendid. Madame Dupris may claim the design, but I know you put in the best touches. The dances and music were great fun, and I met this Yankee officer—"

She paused, not sure she wanted to tell even Hannah how that stranger had affected her. "But," she went on quickly, "then the whole city erupted, after the signing of the Secession Ordinance, and everyone forgot about our party. Just fancy, I heard over three thousand men came to the Institute Hall to witness the signing, and the crowd grew even larger as they marched through the streets."

"I saw the mob from the upper floor," Hannah said. "I never heard so much noise, all the cheering and fireworks. I was afraid they'd set the shop on fire."

Elizabeth glanced at her. "What do you think of this business of secession?"

Instead of answering right away, Hannah look sober. "Some people speak of war. Do you think it will come?"

It was Elizabeth's turn to feel perplexed. "Stephen Hall says the Yankees will never fight. It will be all angry words and gestures. But he's joined a militia unit, just the same."

"Yes," Hannah said. "I've seen some of these new units on parade—a fine bunch they are, playing at soldiers. They can't even march in step."

Elizabeth laughed. "I think they're more concerned with the cut of their uniforms," she agreed. "I've just been to see Stephen getting fitted for a uniform. He's strutting like a young rooster."

They had been strolling through the streets, admiring a handsome Christmas wreath on a shop door and a display of new kid gloves in a shop window. Occasionally they passed a vegetable woman or a cart with its owner hawking wares. But now a new, strident sound interrupted their quiet talk. Elizabeth looked up. She immediately wished she'd minded her steps more carefully, going in any direction but this.

They were approaching a slave mart. An auction was being held in a narrow side street. Standing on a crudely fashioned wooden platform was a black woman of mature years, with a girl clinging to her, a girl younger than Hannah and Elizabeth.

A crowd of white men watched objectively, as if weighing pigs or judging the soundness of a horse's limbs.

"Please, sir," the black woman cried out, her voice heavy with pain. "Not without my baby. She's a hard worker, I swears it. Please, take my girl, too!"

Elizabeth felt her stomach clench. Most plantation owners tried not to separate families, or so it was said. But sometimes what her father called "economic realities" interfered.

Two men pulled the dark-skinned woman and the girl apart. Both were sobbing bitterly. Elizabeth had glimpsed slave markets before, but never so close. She though she would be ill. Then she felt Hannah tremble beside her, and she cursed her own stupidity. If she found this scene upsetting, how would Hannah feel?

"Come away," Elizabeth whispered. "There's nothing we can do."

They hurried back the way they had come. They walked silently, now, and Hannah's face was streaked with tears.

"I'm so sorry," Elizabeth told her. "We should have come this way."

Wiping her cheeks, Hannah didn't answer.

When they parted at the dressmaker's shop, Elizabeth pressed Hannah's hand. "Madame Corday had plans for us on Christmas day, so I won't be able to see you tomorrow. Have a good Christmas, Hannah."

"I will." Hannah managed a smile. "Madame is dining with friends, and Maizie and I will have the day for ourselves. Thank you for the dress goods and the shawl."

"I'll see you soon," Elizabeth promised, then she headed back toward the Academy, walking swiftly over the cobblestone streets. But she avoided the side street with the slave market, trying to blot out the memory of the painful scene they'd witnessed.

Stephen Hall had said that the Southern economy couldn't survive without slavery. Elizabeth thought with a pang of guilt of her own plantation home in Virginia, the big house with its white Ionic columns and spacious rooms. It was easy to pretend, when she saw slaves singing as they planted the fields and women smiling as they cooked, that the system wasn't so bad. Her father said slavery was mentioned in the Bible, as if that made it all right. But the inhumanity of the slave auction was impossible to ignore–humans being sold like animals, families torn apart. Elizabeth remembered her brother's words and whispered to herself, "Does having a darker skin make you less human?"

She shivered. The wind was rising as the sun sank lower in the afternoon sky, but Elizabeth knew the true chill was inside her.

When they retired for bed that night, after Madame led them in a special Christmas prayer and Bible reading, Elizabeth found it hard to sleep. The scene at the slave mart still haunted her. If only they hadn't walked that way. Yet would ignoring it have been any better? The slave auctions would still exist, even if Elizabeth looked the other way.

She sat up quietly in bed and reached for her journal in the table drawer. Lighting her candle, she wrote in its flickering glow.

*Slavery seems wrong to me, but most everyone takes it for granted. Father would say what I think doesn't matter, but Madame Corday believes women should their own opinions. One thing I do know, Hannah is more than property.*

She put away the book, snuffed out her light, and turned restlessly in her bed until a muffled whimper caught her attention.

Across the room, she saw Rosamund push the bedcovers away and reach for a shawl. "I think it's coming from Victorine's room. Do you think she's ill?"

Elizabeth got out of bed and lit a candle. They tiptoed into the hall. The house was dark, the other rooms quiet. But the soft sobs continued.

"Should I call Madame?" Rosamund murmured?

"Let's check first." Elizabeth tapped on the door. "Victorine?"

The noise stopped. In a moment Victorine opened the door. Their usual serene classmate had wet cheeks. Even in the dim candlelight, Elizabeth could tell her friend's eyelids were swollen and red.

"What's wrong?"

Victorine bit her lip. "I'm sorry. I didn't mean to wake you. It's just that I feel so alone tonight. It's the first time I've ever been away from home at Christmas. Even though I attended Madame Corday's school last year, I was able to go home for the holidays."

At her motion, they followed her into the bedroom. Elizabeth put down the candle. "You're homesick?"

Victorine gulped back a sob. "It's silly, *n'est-ce pas*? But—"

Rosamund interrupted. "It's not silly at all. I'm been feeling low, myself. Last Christmas I cried into my pillow, too."

Shivering, Victorine climbed back into her bed. She pulled a coverlet around her shoulders. Elizabeth and Rosamund scrambled onto the foot of the bed and curled up on top of the feather mattresses.

"My maman used to read the Christmas story to us, just as Madame did," Victorine told them. "Papa and Maman and my little sister and I—we'd all go to mass together. And our home in the *Vieux Carre* would be decorated for the *Noel* with pretty glass ball and candles, all smelling of pine boughs. We opened our big gifts on New Year's Day. Marie and I would tear into our boxes—she got a doll with a china head three years ago. I had a new fur tippet. Maman and Papa would sit side by side and hold hands, smiling as we exclaimed over our gifts."

Elizabeth felt a pang of envy. "How nice your family sounds."

Victorine sobbed. "No longer. The last time I saw my maman, she was discolored by the awful yellow fever. They lined the coffin with white silk, but it could not hide the unhealthy flush. When the church bells rang, I kept hoping I would somehow wake and it would all be a nightmare—my mother, my little sister, taken ill and gone so quickly."

Elizabeth felt her own eyes fill in sympathy. "Oh, Victorine, why didn't you tell us before?" She leaned across the bed to hug the weeping girl, and Rosamund put an arm around her from the other side.

"I didn't want to talk about it," Victorine told them, still sobbing. "Papa sent me away to Charleston to be safe from the fever, but I miss home so much, and my maman. And now it's not safe here, either, with all this silly talk of war."

Elizabeth couldn't think what to say. The fears that emerged after the lights were out, the nightmares you didn't want to face—how did you fight them?

"I miss my family, *aussi*," Rosamund said slowly. "I can't help but think of how their Christmas morning will be without me. You know my pa was been in bed for years, brain strokes, the doctor says. He can't walk or hardly talk anymore. Our neighbors say my ma is a saint, taking care of him the way she does, and running the farm. Of course, my brothers also work hard."

Victorine's sobs had eased, and she listened to Rosamund eagerly. "Tell me about your brothers. I wish I had one."

"Strong and sweet-natured, both of them," Rosamund said proudly. "My younger brother had a cough, Ma said in her last letter, but he's taking honey and whiskey for it. My older brother

Daniel is as stout as an oak tree, a pillar of strength. He always makes me feel safe. I think Daniel is sweet on a local girl, but he hasn't told her. I warned him she'll find another beau if he doesn't speak soon. I thought about them all today, wondered if the pond has frozen over and if they've gone ice skating yet."

"I've never skated on a frozen pond." Victorine managed a smile. "New Orleans is not cold enough for water to freeze."

"It snowed in Virginia, my brother said in his Christmas note," Elizabeth said quickly, happy to see their friend distracted from her grief. "It made me remember how Hannah and I used to make snowmen. One Christmas Auntie Mary made us gingerbread men, with raisins for their eyes and mouths. I burned my fingers because I couldn't wait for them to cool."

The other girls laughed.

"We had sugar-coated *beignets* to eat before bedtime, and Maman would tell us a story," Victorine told them, her voice wavering.

"Ma told us stories, too," Rosamund said. "And Ma makes the best molasses cookies, and tea cakes–big cookies, really. I've missed them since I came to Charleston."

"Why did you leave the farm?" Victorine asked.

Rosamund flushed. "I've always loved reading, learning. Uncle Tyrone–he's not really my uncle, but he's been a friend of Ma and Pa's for so long–he lent me books. He used to be a minister. Then–I haven't told you this–he talked Ma into letting him help pay to send me here.

"The Academy was like a dream–whole rooms filled with books, Madame to tell us about her travels in London and Paris and Rome. And Charleston is beautiful, with its lectures and concerts. But sometimes I feel I don't belong. I'm not rich, like y'all. And I miss my family, especially my father. I just hope he understands why I've gone, and doesn't think I don't love him anymore."

This time she was the one whose voice broke, and the other two hugged her.

"We have each other," Elizabeth said, finally. "You are not alone, Victorine, nor are you, Rosamund. We can survive anything if we have friends beside us."

They talked quietly for a few more minutes, then hugged one last time in the candle-lit darkness before Elizabeth and Rosamund hurried back to their warm beds.

## Chapter Five

"It was a wonderful Christmas," Rosamund said as they dressed on the morning of December 26. "The only thing missing was my family. But I do love my gifts."

Reverently, she touched the slim volume of poetry she'd received from Madame Corday, then the silk scarf from Victorine, and the box of chocolates from Elizabeth.

"Yes," Elizabeth agreed. "I love my copy of Shakespeare's *Sonnets*. The muffler you knitted for me is so soft and warm. And the perfume smells so nice, Victorine."

Victorine, waiting for them in the doorway, nodded. "And me, my box from Papa, Mr. Keat's poetry from Madame, and your gifts–lovely! I missed my papa, but—" she smiled shyly at them both–"I have my friends, yes?"

"Yes!" Elizabeth said. "Now, let's see why Madame wants us in the drawing room."

December 26 was called Boxing Day in England, Madame told them, a day for visiting with friends. "It's a custom I like to keep. As my older students, would you three help receive friends and neighbors who come to call?"

Elizabeth agreed politely, although her spirits sank. She had hoped to walk into town to see Hannah. But it would have seemed churlish to refuse, especially after Madame's generosity.

So she sat all afternoon in the big drawing room, prim and proper in deep blue silk. Bored beyond words, she poured tea for the guests who came and went, despite lashings of heavy rain that beat upon the window panes.

"Sugar?" she asked politely, picking up the silver tongs.

"Two lumps, please." Mrs. Grogosset accepted the cup. The wife of a Charleston merchant, she had two daughters who lived at home but attended classes at the school, and she was a frequent, if not popular, visitor.

Elizabeth swallowed a yawn. She stared out the tall windows, wishing that the rain would stop and that she could walk in the garden, or even farther, past the tall brick wall. She could glimpse the street through the wrought-iron gates. A carriage rolled by, pulled by glossy chestnut horses. Then two gentlemen, deep in conversation, walked along beneath an umbrella. Meanwhile, a man tacked a leaflet to the sapling by the street.

"Such a fuss," Mrs. Grosgosset was saying. "My whole household is in an uproar. They searched the back gardens all along our street and found nothing. Anyone fool enough to tie up a slave, especially one who's just been sold, with a rope instead of chains, has to expect a runaway."

Elizabeth sat up straighter. A runaway?

"A shame that your neighbor disturbed your Christmas," Madame Corday said, and then as if trying to change the subject, "How is your younger boy doing with his studies?"

But Mrs. Grosgosset wasn't to be diverted. "The girl was born and raised on Hasler's plantation down by the river. Of course she can't go back there. Any slave who helped her would be beaten within an inch of his life. And she wouldn't know anywhere else to go, so she won't get far. They don't have much intelligence, these creatures."

Fanny had brought in a new plate of cakes, and she leaned over the seated women.

"When that mulatto my husband bought tried to run away, my husband gave him twenty lashes," their guest told them, examining the sweetmeats with a critical eye. She selected a slice of plum cake, adding, "and just a bit of that one, too. Such a nuisance. I thought his back would never heal."

Fanny's hand trembled as she doled out the slices. Elizabeth drew a deep breath, wishing she could shake the plump matron in her lime green silks.

"You can leave the cakes, Fanny," Madame Corday murmured. The black woman left the room quickly. Mrs.

Grosgosset stirred her tea, rattling the china cup in its saucer and took another big bite of cake, apparently unaware of the currents of tension stirring in the room.

Madame Corday reached for a thin periodical. "Have you seen the newest fashions from the Continent? Some very daring bonnets this season."

Talk turned to ostrich plumes and scalloped flounces, and Elizabeth's thoughts wandered again. She wished she were having tea with Adam Cranfield instead of Mrs. Grosgosset. He would walk into the drawing room, bow low over her hand, present her with a large bouquet of flowers—no, a single rosebud—and those deep, dark eyes would sparkle as he murmured into her ear. "I haven't been able to forget you, Miss Stafford. You've shadowed my days and haunted my nights, leaving me no peace until I could see you again."

No, he wouldn't make pretty speeches. He'd said as much the night of the Christmas Ball. Elizabeth sighed, wishing for the hundredth time that they hadn't been interrupted by the tumult of the signing of the Ordinance of Secession. He had been standing so close. If they had been alone, would he have bent forward, daring to touch his lips to her own? She felt butterflies in her stomach just dreaming of the possibility.

"Miss Elizabeth, a note for you from Madame Dupris." Fanny stood in the doorway.

Startled, Elizabeth excused herself and hurried into the hallway. She accepted the folded sheet of paper Fanny held out and scanned it.

*Please send Hannah back by nightfall,* the cramped handwriting said. *I have need of her, and a half-day's holiday is enough.* It was signed by the modiste.

Elizabeth blinked. Madame Dupris thought Hannah was here? But she hadn't come. Where was she?

Elizabeth's throat felt tight, as if unseen fingers gripped it. It seemed hard to take a breath. Why had Hannah gone off like this, deceiving her employer, pretending that she was going to see Elizabeth? Hannah could be mistaken for a runaway, and they both knew what happened to runaway slaves.

Elizabeth crumpled the paper between suddenly damp palms. What could she do?

"Who brought this?" she almost whispered to Fanny.

"Maizie. She's waiting at the back door."

"I see. Tell Maizie to say to Madame Dupris that I will send Hannah back presently. I need her to assist me in a fitting, but we'll be done soon."

Fanny looked perplexed, but she didn't argue. Watching her retreating toward the back door, Elizabeth tried to think.

Rosamund came into the hall, her blue eyes troubled. "What is it, Elizabeth? You're pale as bleached cotton."

"A message from the shop where Hannah is employed–she's missing. I don't know what's wrong," Elizabeth explained. "I have to find out—Hannah might be in danger. Don't tell anyone."

"But what about Madame Corday?"

"Tell her I had to lie down. She knows what I think of Mrs. Grosgosset. Maybe she'll think I developed a nervous headache."

Rosamund shook her head. "You can't go out now, Elizabeth. It's almost dark."

"I must. I'll be back as soon as I can." Elizabeth ran lightly up the stairs, found a warm shawl and a thicker soled pair of shoes, and tiptoed down the back staircase. She avoided the front hall, where she would have had to pass the parlor doorway. This was no time to catch Madame Corday's eye.

She went down the back hall instead and slipped out the door into the garden. The rain had stopped, although puddles covered the hard packed earth. She ran past the kitchen house and stole out through the rear gate.

This gate, too, would be locked when the sun set, but she would worry about that later. The winter sun was low in the sky and the air cool and damp against her face.

Elizabeth walked through the fading light, surveying the street with an anxious gaze. Where could Hannah have gone, and why? She had never done anything like this before.

A fluttering leaflet on a tree caught Elizabeth's atention. She stopped to read the heavy print.

ESCAPED SLAVE GIRL

AGE FOURTEEN, HEIGHT 5'2" FIGURE SLIM

PROPERTY OF ABRAM McCOLLISTER, INQUIRE

AT MILLS HOTEL. REWARD

Elizabeth shivered. Was this the same girl they'd seen at the slave auction? Hannah had been upset over the incident. Was there any connection between the runaway and Hannah's sudden absence?

Once out of sight of the Academy, Elizabeth combed the streets between the school and the shop belonging to Hannah's employer. Night came on rapidly. The gloomy streets were lit by flickering rays from the gas street lamps and faint light escaping through lace-curtained windows. Tendrils of fog hugged the pavement.

She smelled the tang of sea air and turn instinctively toward the harbor. After another block, she could hear the crash of waves against the rocks below the seawall, and the raucous cry of seagulls wheeling overhead. Elizabeth walked along the deserted harbor for a way, left the seawall and stepped onto the damp sand and rocks, feeling shells crunch beneath her soles.

She didn't know what to do. If Madame Corday had discovered her absence, Elizabeth would already be in trouble, and she'd done nothing help her childhood companion. What would happen to Hannah if she was discovered out past the curfew? Oh, where could she be?

Elizabeth glanced toward the water. Castle Pinckney on its island was the closest fortification, Fort Moultrie was to the left, and the unfinished Fort Sumter was a small hump in the center of the harbor. State patrol boats passed occasionally, and a dark shape rode the crest of the waves in the moonlight. But Hannah would not have any access to a boat, and why should she want to, anyhow?

Deep in thought, Elizabeth stared out to sea, hardly noticing the splash of oars over the pounding waves. Then a dark form rose up in front of her. A strong pair of hands grabbed her shoulders.

Cold with fear, Elizabeth tried to scream.

A hand covered her mouth—an arm encircled her firmly. "I didn't think you were so easily frightened, Miss Stanford," a familiar voice said.

Her breath steadied as she gazed up at the face so close to her own. She could make out masculine features now—heavy brows and a pair of dark eyes mocking her. Her fear vanished. For an instant she felt an almost irresistible attraction. Then the hardness of his tone reached her, and her emotions changed as swiftly as the flicker of his eyes.

Anger washed through her. Elizabeth had dreamed of another meeting between them ever since the Christmas Ball, but not like this.

She stepped back as he dropped his constraining hand. "This is fine gentlemanly conduct—grabbing hold of me like a brigand? What are you doing here, Lieutenant Cranfield?"

"I could ask the same of you. Does Madame Corday allow her charges to roam the harbor at night?" His broad shoulders hid the ocean from her view, and his blue uniform merged with the darkness.

Again she fought the wish to find herself in his embrace. His arrogance fueled her anger, masking her conflicting emotions.

"It's no business of yours! I should think you'd have concerns of your own, sir, with all this talk in town of war, and secession a reality."

"Impetuous, these South Carolinians," he muttered, his tone mocking her once again. "It's all hot air, I suspect. Everyone knows Southerners are puffed up with their own bravado."

"I wouldn't underestimate the South, Lieutenant." Elizabeth hugged her shawl closer. "We might surprise you one day. Why aren't you out there guarding your fort? Mr. Hall tells me the cows wander in and out at will. A fine place it will be to defend, if you should need to."

"Are the females of Charleston studying military tactics, now? A sad waste of such an admirable lady's time."

"If you find me admirable, why haven't you come to call?" she snapped, then paused, aghast at having betrayed her feelings.

To her horror, he laughed out loud. "I won't deny that I was tempted. But I know better. You're all alike, you Southern women. Vain as little Eves, scheming as little Delilahs. My own mother seduced my father, promised to love him forever and follow him anywhere, then spent the rest of her life bemoaning her exile from family and friends. She found New England too cold, too unfriendly, too harsh for her frail Virginia blood. My father paid the price, and so did I, growing up haunted by her sad plaints. It taught me a lesson about women, especially Southern women."

Elizabeth felt a wave of anger so overwhelming that she could hardly see. A dark cloud seemed to blur her vision. "How dare you! Whatever your mother did, you know nothing about me."

"I see you're scheming to use your beauty just as she did. Are you out to meet your lover–the fine Confederate gentleman with the carefully combed fair hair? Who would dare a night like this unless their hearts were on romance?"

"I was not meeting a lover!" Elizabeth could hardly force out the words through jaws tight with fury. Then she realized her mistake, even as she saw his eyes narrow in puzzlement.

"Then why—"

"It's nothing to you."

He mustn't suspect why she was combing Charleston at night, all alone. Hannah might suffer for it. But he frowned at her as if deep in thought. Trying to divert him, she continued her tirade.

"You Yankees are all pigheaded and overbearing. I've heard as much, and now I know it to be true." She folded her arms as if in disgust, trying not to reveal her apprehension. Her hands were trembling. The breeze from the ocean was cold and damp. Despite her best efforts, she shivered. Faint sounds from the harbor nudged at her attention, but she was too absorbed in her war of words with the lieutenant to pay heed.

"If your headmistress can't keep you indoors, I think someone needs to exercise some control," the arrogant young officer continued. "I should do your Carolina cavalier a favor and warn him now. You prance and snort like a fine filly, Miss Stafford, but even the most spirited young horse must be broken."

"If I'm ever reined in, it will not be by a man who compares me to a brute animal," Elizabeth retorted, infuriated by his icy self-control. She had hungered to hear his voice again, and now he could only berate her. She felt sick at heart, and her disappointment fueled her anger.

Lowering the heavy shawl that had been wrapped around her face for warmth she lifted her chin. "It will be by a better man than you, sir!"

He stepped forward and gripped her shoulders once more. This time, she could tell that he was breathing quickly. Somewhere deep inside, she felt pleasure. He might still feign indifference, but she could feel the spark of answering emotion. She had finally pierced his armor.

"Your Charleston beau, no doubt? And what should I compare you to, then?"

"Nothing." Elizabeth met his steady gaze without dropping his own. His grip on his shoulders did not loosen. She could have sworn his fingers would burn through the heavy fabric of her clothing and sear her skin. "I am only myself."

"True enough. I take back what I said. You may be a Southern vixen, but I've never met another woman quite like you." He bent closer, and Elizabeth felt her pulse pound within her temples. Dipped in concentration, his brows formed a dark shadow across his face.

She couldn't discern the expression in his deep brown eyes through the darkness, but she could hear him breathing fast and hard. Then she felt his lips firm and cool against her own, tasting of salt. The blood pounded in her ears. She forgot how to think and only feelings swept through her–

How long the kiss lasted, Elizabeth never knew. Years, mayhap. It seemed forever. She'd never been kissed like this. Proper young ladies weren't.

When he released her at last, both were breathing fast, and her knees felt weak. Afraid she might fall, she clung to his arm a moment longer.

She had long forgotten her surroundings, her mission, her fears. Slowly it all came back. She heard the splash of waves against the rocks, but the other sound–the light noise that had been added to the usual rise and fall of the water, the gulls' cries, and the faint city noises behind them–was gone. Finally, she realized what it had been: the sound of rowing, of rough, uneven rowing by men unaccustomed to such a task, soldiers recast as seamen.

As if to confirm her intuition, a faint whistle sounded from the water's edge, followed by a male voice.

"Cranfield, they're safely past. Come on, man. If Captain Doubleday finds out how far we came, or Major Anderson—perish the thought—we'll be in hot water for sure."

Anger gave Elizabeth renewed strength. She straightened, her back erect once more, and glared at the young officer.

"You're moving troops out there, aren't you?"

"Studying military tactics again, Miss Stanford?" The mocking tone was back.

"Your chicanery was merely to deceive me, to distract me from paying heed to the harbor. You are a cad, sir!"

"Just doing my duty, ma'am," he told her, his tone a shade too solemn. "As you suggested."

She thought she heard the hint of laughter in his voice, but it only increased her anger.

"You are no gentleman, Lieutenant Cranfield." She stamped her feet in the damp sand, and shells crackled. "I hope never to see you again!"

"If the governor of South Carolina has his way, your wish will likely be granted."

"Cranfield, come on!"

The soft call from the beach made him turn. But he hesitated, looking back at Elizabeth. She thought he made motion as if to reach once more for her hand, but he drew back and gave her a formal bow, instead.

"Your servant, ma'am. I must leave you now. I assume that whoever you came to meet will see you safely home."

She bit back an unladylike oath. "Get out of my sight!"

He ran lightly to the water's edge. She heard the grating sound as he pushed the boat off the sand into the water. Then he climbed into the small rowboat, and she heard only the sound of oars as it moved away.

Shivering, Elizabeth drew her shawl around her. For the first time, she felt something hard inside her still clenched fist. She opened her fingers slowly. It was a small brass button—her angry grip had somehow pulled it from the lieutenant's uniform. She raised her hand to cast it aside like the faithless Yankee himself, then paused. Instead, she tucked it carefully inside her bodice-next to her heart.

But she was damp from the sea breeze and no closer to finding Hannah than when she had left the school grounds. Madame Corday would be aghast if she discovered Elizabeth's absence at such an hour, and the modiste would be furious that Hannah had not returned.

Feeling thoroughly defeated, Elizabeth retraced her steps. Her skirts were wet and splashed with mud, and the wind cut through her shawl.

When she neared the Academy, Elizabeth realized the extent of her own predicament. Both gates would be locked. She would have to ring the bell to get in or huddle in the cold beneath a tree all night. What would Madame say? Would the headmistress send Elizabeth home in disgrace? This escapade was more than enough to ensure endless gossip, tarnishing any girl's reputation for life.

Not that she'd been up to anything unseemly, Elizabeth told herself. She hadn't *planned* to meet the infuriating lieutenant. If their meeting had been like the ones she had dreamed of, it might have been worth her disgrace.

But he had turned a dream into a nightmare with his mocking words, his contradictory actions. To Hades with him, she thought. But she could still feel his grip on her shoulders, his lips firm against hers, and the brass button pressed hard against her skin.

She had almost reached the back gate when she stepped on a fallen tree twig. It cracked beneath her feet, and Elizabeth heard the sound of a gasp from behind a thick oak tree.

"Who is it?" She hissed, her heart pounding.

"Miss Elizabeth?" The voice was faint.

"Hannah?" Elizabeth's fear and relief turned abruptly to anger. She hurried around the tree. "What in heaven's name have you been up to? Going off without any word–I could have you whipped!"

Silence, then a small sigh from the darkness. "Yes," Hannah said softly. "Yes, Miss Elizabeth, you could."

An old memory, long suppressed, rose unbidden. A midwinter day, with frost lingering on a few faded corn stalks. Elizabeth had escaped her tutor and run out into the edge of the fields where the slave cabins huddled.

One of the field hands was being beaten–she didn't remember why. But the blood dripping down the torn flesh of his back, the dark skin scored with scarlet welts as he moaned with each lash of the heavy leather whip, was a sight she could never forget. Elizabeth felt a wave of nausea and pushed the image to the back of her mind. Guilt rushed up, and with it came deep contrition.

"I didn't mean it, Hannah. You know I didn't. I was so worried! If you'd been caught away from your shop—"

"I wasn't," Hannah whispered.

She sounded weary beyond words. Elizabeth reached for the other girl, touching Hannah's face in the darkness. She felt dampness, smelled an acrid scent. "There's blood on your cheek!" She could detect Hannah's shivers.

"It's nothing. I walked into a tree branch."

"What were you doing, Hannah. Where have you been?" The light from the house past the wall hardly touched them. Elizabeth tried to see the other's face, but the night was too dark.

"I can't tell you, Lizbet. Please don't ask me," Hannah answered, her voice soft.

It was a name from their shared childhood, from the long-ago time when Hannah and Lizbet had been, in their own innocent eyes, truly equal.

Until tonight, Elizabeth had hardly realized how far they had come or how widely their paths had diverged. She swallowed hard. She had every right–every legal right–to know all of Hannah's movements. She was Hannah's mistress, her owner in all but actual title, which her father held. . . But she could beat her, sell her, kill her, and no law would interfere. Elizabeth had come face to face with the slave mart all over again.

But Hannah was not just another dark face, another nameless slave on a big plantation. Hannah was the child she had shared tea cakes with, the girl she had whispered secrets to, the friend who had always been loyal. Hannah was her first and best friend, almost her sister.

This was what her brother John had meant, then, about slavery not being right. For the first time Elizabeth understood, really understood, the truth of his quiet words, not just with her mind but with her heart.

A dozen questions about Hannah's actions rose inside her. She thought of the young escaped slave, of the beatings and hangings and death that came to those who aided runaways. Had Hannah. . . . . With difficulty, Elizabeth pushed all the questions back. It was the hardest thing she had ever done.

"We must get you cleaned up and back to Madame Dupris's," she murmured. "But I don't know how I'm going to get inside."

She walked to the back gate and touched the wood frame gently. To her amazement, the gate moved under her hand. She pushed it open and almost fell over the dark shape waiting just beyond.

"Oh, Fanny, is that you?"

"I be waiting for you, Miss Elizabeth. Madame don't know," Fanny whispered. She stared through the darkness. "Who d'at?"

"It's Hannah. She just—" Elizabeth stopped, not knowing what excuse to make.

But Fanny didn't ask. She led them up the path to the shadowed kitchen house. While they crouched on the brick hearth, Fanny stirred the coals and lit one tallow candle.

Wrinkling her nose at the candle's strong odor, Elizabeth washed Hannah's face with cold water and tried to think of some kind of plan.

"I need paper and ink," she told them. "Wait here and don't make any noise."

She tiptoed into the main house–Fanny had contrived to leave the side door unlocked–and through the hall to the large schoolroom where she found a sheet of paper and a pen and inkwell. Her heart beat fast as she listened for any sounds from above, but the house was dark and seemed to sleep with the rest of its inhabitants.

Back in the cold kitchen, she leaned over the rough-hewn table and scribbled a hasty note.

"I'm telling her that you fell off a stool while doing my fitting and have lain in a swoon for several hours. That will explain why you look so drawn and weak," Elizabeth explained. "If she questions you, tell her it was my carelessness and to see me if she wants to complain."

Hannah pressed Elizabeth's hand as she put the note into her apron pocket. "This will do, I think. You always could talk your way out of a scrape better than anyone."

Impulsively, Elizabeth hugged her. They clung together for a moment, then she urged Hannah gently toward the back gate. "We'd better go. It's late, and there's the curfew."

They walked side by side through the dark streets to the shop. "Thank you, Elizabeth,"

Hannah said, her voice low. Then she disappeared into the shop. Elizabeth waited to be sure the dressmaker accepted their story, then hurried back to the school.

Suddenly feeling exhausted, herself, she locked the side door and made her way up the staircase to her room.

She eased the bedroom door open, slipped in and shut it behind her. Across the room, Rosamund sat up in bed.

"Elizabeth! Are you all right?"

"Yes." Elizabeth fumbled with her buttons and hooks in the darkness, dropping her damp garments to the floor. She would give them to Fanny to wash in the morning. "Does Madame know I've been gone?"

"No, I told her you were asleep already, and she didn't check your bed, thank goodness. I was so worried. What about Hannah? Did you find her? Where did you go?"

"All's well. But it's a long story, and I'm too tired." Elizabeth crawled into bed with her nightgown unbuttoned. The story would have to be somewhat abridged, she thought. She would gather her thoughts tomorrow. No need to shock Rosamund with her scandalous adventure–especially the part concerning the lieutenant's kiss! Placing his button carefully beneath her pillow, she touched her lips once more, as if the touch of his embrace still lingered. Then sleep overcame her.

They were at breakfast when an agitated neighbor rang the front bell with the news. The other girls buzzed with excitement, but Elizabeth bent over her porridge without speaking as she listened to breathless snatches of talk.

"Smoke across the harbor–Fort Moultrie burning–the cannons spiked–all the Yankee troops moved themselves to Fort Sumter–our South Carolina guard boats completely evaded!"

The adults conferred, heads close, and Madame's response was spoken too low for Elizabeth to overhear.

"What does it mean?" Rosamund asked her friend, her brow furrowed with worry.

Elizabeth shook her head and didn't answer. But when the neighbor, fortified with a strong cup of tea, had at last departed, and the other girls had been shooed toward the schoolrooms, she stayed long enough to repeat the question to Madame Corday.

The headmistress pushed a chair back into place under the dining table, her expression distracted. "I fear we are one step closer to war."

# Chapter Six

"Isn't this fun?" Victorine slanted her parasol carefully to guard her perfect complexion from the March sunlight. Watching a seagull swoop low over Charleston Harbor, Elizabeth nodded. She gripped the sides of her wooden seat and fought to control her queasy stomach as they swayed and dipped in the small boat. The breeze on her face helped. It was fresh and cool and smelled of the sea.

"It was very kind of Mr. Hall to obtain a permit to allow us to visit Sullivan's Island," Rosamund added. "Of course,"–she lowered her voice mischievously–"I think he would do anything to spend time with a certain student."

They both grinned at Elizabeth, who only shrugged her shoulders. It was wonderful to be free of the schoolroom on such a lovely spring Saturday. But her first rush of excitement at the excursion had subsided. The differences already visible in Charleston were shocking.

The short boat ride had given them all a good look at how their city had changed in the last three months. Earth embankments thrown up at the end of the peninsula blocked the sea view of spacious summer homes. Cannons were manned in the park. The wharves around the harbor bustled with men in colorful uniforms. Some guard boats patrolled the harbor regularly, as everyone waited to see how the Northern government would respond to South Carolina's secession.

As if Rosamund had read her thoughts, she said, "Don't the Zouaves have exotic uniforms! Those scarlet caps and baggy trousers–they could have stepped out of an Arabian fairy tale. But I think Mr. Hall's unit looks much more distinguished."

She gave Elizabeth another sidelong glance. Elizabeth merely nodded, refusing to rise to the bait. She knew her friends were curious as to the extent of her feelings for Stephen Hall, but she was quite prepared to leave them in the dark. She couldn't tell them, either, that her thoughts had been of only one man over the past few months—a tall, dark-haired Yankee soldier.

"They're all so brave, *n'est-ce pas*? I know we'll be safe," Victorine told them, as if trying to reassure herself as much as anyone else. "After all, General Beauregard is in command of the troops now. He's from Louisiana, from a fine Creole family. Did I tell you?"

"Only about three times a day," Rosamund answered cheerfully. "Look at the pelican diving for a fish."

When the short cruise ended, they lifted their skirts as they disembarked at Sullivan's Island. Stephan Hall was waiting. He handed them all up into the wagon, careful of their hoopskirts.

"Good morning, Madame Corday," he said. "I'm so happy you could come. Miss LaGrande, Miss Brigham."

When's Elizabeth's turn came, he held her hand a moment too long, and she blushed. "Miss Elizabeth," he said, his grin widening. "I'm so happy to see you."

She looked away from his merry blue eyes, afraid they would reveal his true feelings if she looked too closely.

She turned and stepped up into the wagon, taking one of the rough-hewn seats. She took her time arranging her skirts and adjusting her bonnet to shade her face from the sun. Fortunately, Stephen had assumed his role as guide and was pointing out fortifications to Madame Corday.

When they reached Fort Moultrie, now manned by South Carolina troops, they stopped and walked through the old fort. The small fortification hadn't changed very much since the American Revolution, Stephen told them. Walls of palmetto logs held back the wind-blown sand on one side. Other walls were brick and stone. The cannons spiked by Major Anderson's Union forces on their withdrawal to Fort Sumter had been repaired or replaced.

The Revolution had brought the states together to make one nation, Elizabeth couldn't help thinking. If this really came to war, would it tear that hard-won nation apart? The sun was warm overhead, the sea breeze cool on her face. It was a day for pleasant excursions, not for talk of war. Elizabeth found the whole scene a little unreal.

And yet young men in varied, sometimes fantastic, uniforms manned fortifications, and scores of small tents stretched across the island.

When they reached Stephen Hall's own encampment, he helped them down from the wagon. They had brought along baskets of food, Madame sensibly not trusting menfolk to come up with edible foodstuffs. They sat on logs and rough wooden chairs as Madame passed around cold chicken and small pork pies, fruit, and pastry. Stephen helped give everyone lemonade in tin cups.

"Roughing it, I see," Elizabeth told him, keeping her tone merry. She tasted her lemonade. It was not quite sweet enough, but she wouldn't have dreamed of remarking upon its deficiencies. He was too proud of his role as host.

"That's the way it is for soldiers," he said, his tone almost bragging. "I'll have you know I'm currying my own horse these days. I sent my groom back home to the plantation."

It was said with so much pride that Elizabeth swallowed her giggle.

"I think that's marvelous," Victorine said, seriously. "And the whole senior class at Charleston College taking a leave of absence to sign up—a magnificent gesture!"

"We couldn't let the Citadel cadets get all the glory. They were so lucky, firing on the *Star of the West* in January, turning back a ship full of reinforcements and supplies for Sumter. But we'll do our share, don't you worry."

"I still hope it doesn't come to actual fighting," soft-hearted Rosamund murmured.

"Lincoln has no stomach for war–look at how he's delaying," Stephen told them, his fair skin flushed from excitement as well as perpetual sunburn. "Especially after other states have seceded, too. South Carolina's not alone anymore. Mississippi, Florida, Alabama, Georgia."

"Louisiana," Victorine added loyally.

"Yes, and Texas, also. The Confederate States are well on their way. I mean, President Jeff Davis's already inaugurated. Other states will join us, wait and see."

Rosamund looked troubled. "Tennessee voted down the first secession vote. But my mother says in her letters that they're still wrangling."

"It will all be over by the end of the summer," Stephen told them, taking a hearty bite from his pork pie. "They say Sumter's almost out of food. We'll starve them out in no time. They have little coal left to burn, and it gets cold out here at night, with the wind off the sea."

"Really?" Elizabeth put down her piece of chicken, her appetite fading. She had a disquieting image of Adam Cranfield, cold and hungry but too proud to surrender even if he had the chance. She tried to push the picture away, fixing her gaze on Stephen's cheerful face.

"The papers said last week that Sumter is to be evacuated," Stephen reminded them. "Didn't I say the Yankees would never fight? A shame, really. All this drilling for nothing. We'd have shown them what we can do." He brushed a speck off his immaculate uniform.

Elizabeth couldn't help glancing out over the harbor. "A pity someone hasn't informed Major Anderson, then," she said. But she silently wondered: What are those men thinking, holed up on that little island fortress? What does Adam Cranfield feel, right now?

"My parents were proud of me for taking leave from the college," Stephen told them. "Look at our new flag. My sisters sewed it themselves for our unit."

They all stared at the flag snapping in the brisk wind. A white palmetto tree and crescent showed bright against a blue background. The Stars and Stripes would not fly over Charleston again, Elizabeth thought, not unless the city was conquered. It was all so strange.

"Would you walk a little way with me, Miss Elizabeth?" Stephen asked hopefully.

Elizabeth glanced at Madame Corday, who had been talking quietly to another young officer. Madame nodded.

"Not too far," the headmistress said.

Elizabeth put her hand through Stephen's arm. They left the tents behind and strolled over the hand-packed sand.

"Are you proud of me?" Stephen asked, peering beneath her bonnet's brim to see her face.

Elizabeth, who knew she'd been silent too long, flashed him a bright smile. "Of course I am."

His eyes flashed. "That means more to me than anything, Miss Elizabeth," he told her seriously. "I mean, I would have joined up anyhow, what else could a man of honor do? But if I can make you proud—I'll be a happy man."

Elizabeth looked away from his intense gaze. "How could I not be?" she said, keeping her tone light. "Giving up your studies, your free time, to march and drill and dig fortifications. I'll wager you never dug ditches before."

He shook his head and held out a newly scored palm for her to inspect. "Blisters."

Elizabeth bit back a smile. "Impressive," she agreed, touching his hand softly. This was a tactical mistake. He gripped her hand very tightly and held it.

"But do you feel the kind of pride that a lady feels when she—when they—" He stumbled over his words, squeezing her hand so hard that she winced.

Elizabeth felt trapped. "Don't," she said sharply, pulling her hand out of his grip.

Stephen's smile faded. He looked so crushed that she felt a pang of conscience. Not wanting to see the quick misery in those transparent blue eyes, she looked down.

His gray uniform was trim, the gold braid on his trousers bright. His boots shone, too. They had been blacked and buffed to a high gloss. Despite his blistered hands, he had doubtless done it himself, perhaps for the first time in his life. After a lifetime of pampering, Stephen was growing up. Everyone, everything was changing. Elizabeth felt her head whirl, and she trembled.

"Are you all right?" He gripped her arm again, this time with solicitude. "Is the sun too hot? Shall I take you back? I didn't mean to upset you, Miss Elizabeth."

His tone was so humble, his dejection so apparent that Elizabeth couldn't bear it. He was giving up all his accustomed comfort, preparing to fight, to be shot at, if war finally came. And it might, despite the optimism that still ran high in Charleston. She couldn't wound him like this.

"No, I'm fine," she murmured. "It's just so much—all of this."

"Don't you worry," he assured her eagerly. "You won't be in danger. Shoot, the Yankees will never fight. They're a dull bunch, shopkeepers and factory workers. They're not *gentlemen*."

Everyone in town said that. But the mention of Yankees always reminded Elizabeth of Adam Cranfield, with his quiet resolution, his air of inner certainty. Weren't those qualities also the mark of a gentleman? Of course, he hadn't behaved like a gentleman that long-ago night on the beach. Her heart pounded at the memory.

"We'll protect our ladies and our city," Stephen went on. "That's what we're here for."

"I'm not afraid for myself," Elizabeth said. "But our young men—" She regretted her remark at once because she saw hope reappear in his eyes.

"You do care about me, then! Oh, Miss Elizabeth. Can I hope that someday you'll return my regard?" He captured both her hands this time and turned her to face him.

"Yes, no, I mean, I don't know, Mr. Hall."

Elizabeth wished she didn't feel as if she were kicking an eager puppy. Glancing over her shoulder, she saw they had passed an earthen embankment that hid them briefly from the school party at his camp. She stood on tiptoe and gave him a swift, sisterly kiss on his cheek, hoping to soothe his wounded feelings.

Her gesture succeeded only too well.

"Miss Elizabeth!" Stephen grabbed her in an awkward embrace and kissed her hard on the lips.

Caught by surprise, Elizabeth stood motionless, waiting for the same rush of emotion and exhilaration that she had felt with Lieutenant Cranfield's kiss. But her pulse did not quicken, her knees remained quite firm.

Stephen apparently felt enough emotion for them both. When he released her, his grin was wide and triumphant. "I knew you cared," he exulted. "Oh, Miss Elizabeth! You will wait for me–until I can speak to your father? It surely won't be long until I'm free from my duties."

Alarmed, Elizabeth searched for words. Did Stephen think they were actually engaged? "I—"

"Elizabeth! We have to start back now," Victorine called from behind them.

Elizabeth turned quickly to see Victorine and a young militia member strolling along the sand.

Elizabeth made a face at Stephen. "Hush, not now," she whispered.

He nodded in understanding. "It's our secret," he told her. But he patted her hand as they walked back arm in arm.

She sighed. Now what had she done?

That night, after Rosamund was asleep, Elizabeth kissed the brass button–as she did every evening–then pulled out her journal.

> *Stephen is sweet and his family likes me. My father would approve. We would make a proper match. But Stephen doesn't make my heart beat fast. The room doesn't brighten when he walks in. Yet, am I only drawn to Adam because he's so different? Am I only–*
>
> *as my father would say–being contrary? Is it love or schoolgirl infatuation? How can I know when my whole life hangs in the balance? I wish I knew what to do!*

The next two weeks crawled by. Finally, Elizabeth talked her way into doing errands for Madame one sunny afternoon. But after filling her basket with vegetables at the market, she lingered, not ready to go back.

Housetops were still decorated with palmetto flags and bunting, and a band blared on a street corner. Elizabeth stepped hastily aside to avoid brand-new soldiers drilling. *War fever*, she thought.

Someone touched her arm, and Elizabeth jumped. Turning, she wasn't prepared to see the man who had filled her thoughts, day and night, since that evening on the beach. Adam Cranfield stood before her in his neat blue uniform, his expression hard to read.

"You? What are you doing here." She stepped back, trying to look suitably haughty. He mustn't guess how her stomach knotted just to see him so near. But she couldn't stop herself from memorizing the dark brows, the tiny scar on his chin.

"Fanny told me you were here, Miss Stafford. I fear I own you an apology."

Her blood seemed to roar in her ears. Elizabeth drew a deep breath, feeling slightly dizzy. "Apology? I think not. Some words are beyond apology. Delilah, I think you called me."

He frowned. "Perhaps that was too harsh. But I swore never to fall into the same trap my father did. It's not you. That is—I simply have no place in my life for faint-hearted Southern women."

"Is this an apology or more insults?" She wanted to stamp her feet and scream at him. Yet at the same time, she ached to reach out and wipe away the old pain she saw reflected in his face. Her pride would allow neither.

He flinched, then to her surprise, gripped her hand. She felt herself tremble at his touch.

Perhaps he sensed her tension. He said quickly, "Miss Stafford, I swear I would never harm you. That night on the beach, I wanted to divert your attention, true, but also I couldn't resist the excuse to kiss you." He lowered his voice, and his husky tone sent shivers along Elizabeth's spine. "If I forgot to be a gentleman and remembered only that I am a man, forgive me."

Elizabeth looked up at him. How easy it would be to lean into his arms. "You make it hard for me to remember my duty, or my anger," she murmured. "Perhaps—"

"What this?" A beefy man in a bright purple waistcoat peered at them with ready suspicion. "Is this man accosting you—this *Yankee?*"

Elizabeth blushed. "No, no."

But the man didn't listen. Other men gathered around them, men with angry red faces, eyes bright with antipathy.

Alarmed, Elizabeth whispered to Adam, "You must go, now!"

Surrounded by the ever-growing crowd, the Yankee officer looked grim but not afraid. He gave her a slight bow, as if too much had already been said, and turned away, while the crowd shouted and jeered.

"Northerner! Stay out of our town!"

Badly shaken, Elizabeth hurried back toward the Academy. She must return before Madame wondered about the delay. But she felt hollow inside.

That night she wrote in her journal again.

*Was I wrong to listen to his apology? And is it no longer possible to*

*even speak to a Yankee?*

Inside the safety of the school walls, the girls kept up their routine of study, reading, and needlework, but Madame Corday's expression was grave, and Fanny jumped at every sound. The students, also, seemed edgy.

Despite his military duties, Stephen Hall managed to find the time to smuggle notes into the school. These missives overflowed with sentimental poetry that made Elizabeth want to scream. Even without her recurring memories of Adam, she could not feel easy about Stephen's devotion.

"If he says, 'O, my luve is like a red, red, rose,' one more time, I'm going to stuff the verse back down his throat," Elizabeth said to Rosamund one April afternoon. "Sometimes I think he doesn't even see me, really."

"What do you mean?" Rosamund looked startled.

"Not *me*," Elizabeth tried to explain. "He thinks I'm the beautiful, sweet-natured princess in her tower and he's the handsome young knight, the prince charming. He may love the romance, but he doesn't know the person I am inside—not to mention that I'm not beautiful, and I'm certainly not sweet, not very often, anyhow."

Rosamund laughed, but she sobered quickly.

"You should tell him it's all a mistake," she pointed out, always practical. She dotted an *I* in her essay and blotted the ink carefully so that it wouldn't smudge. "You can't allow him to go on thinking that y'all are betrothed, Elizabeth. It isn't fair."

"I know. I feel like such a fool, getting myself into this tangle." Elizabeth frowned at the book in front of her. She'd read this chapter on Mary, Queen of Scots, twice, unable to concentrate on the small print. "And I hate to wound his feelings."

"Perhaps you care more for him than you want to admit?" Rosamund's blue eyes were clear.

Elizabeth looked away.

"What's this? Talking secrets?" Victorine joined them in the small study, with Sarah behind her.

"Of course not," Elizabeth snapped. "We are discussing the British monarchy."

Victorine shook her head. "*Non*, no more books! We have had enough of that from Madame this morning. Let my tired brain rest. Look, I have a new needlework pattern."

"It's very nice," Sarah put in. "Look how tiny the stitches are. Victorine's needlework is very fine."

"Lovely," Elizabeth agreed, not very interested in plying her needle but happy to change the subject. "And what a nice shade of blue."

Victorine nodded and dropped a skein of the fine thread into Rosamund's lap. "You can use this to finish hemming your handkerchief if you like. I know you ran out of thread last week, and I have more than enough."

"Thank you," Rosamund said, her voice soft, her tone a bit strained. Victorine meant well, Elizabeth thought, but she could be tactless. She didn't have to make Rosamund feel like a charity case.

Victorine threaded her needle with care, then spread out the shawl she was embroidering. The other girls gathered around to examine the delicate stitches. Elizabeth had to admit that the pattern of pink roses against a blue trellis was a pretty one.

"*Voici*–this stitch–she is one my maman taught me," Victorine told them. "She did needlework beyond excellence."

Elizabeth felt a pang of envy. "You were fortunate to know your mother," she murmured. "I don't remember mine."

Victorine nodded. "I have many good memories. My maman was a fine lady. Her ankles and wrists were fine boned and delicate. Her complexion was always white and pure, and she never dirtied her hands or appeared in a soiled gown."

Elizabeth nodded, but Rosamund's face flushed. "Allow me to tell you, Victorine, that I went into the garden this morning to dig new potatoes for Fanny, and I forgot to change my apron."

Elizabeth blinked, surprised by this unusual outburst. She stared at the slight smudge of dirt on the hem of Rosamund's tan-colored apron. She hadn't even noticed. She did know that Rosamund owned only a fraction of the clothing that crowded Victorine's wardrobe. Perhaps there were no more clean aprons to change into.

"You should leave the dirty work to the servants," Victorine answered.

Rosamund's usually even voice trembled with emotion. "I like the feel of clean garden dirt, Victorine, and the smooth skin of tiny potatoes and carrots fresh for the table. It's honest toil. Not everyone lives in a fine New Orleans mansion, protected from every care. Some people work for their dinner."

Victorine stabbed her needle so hard into the delicate silk of her shawl that she winced. She raised her wounded finger to her mouth. "*Mon Dieu*, is your memory so short? My beloved maman lies in a marble vault. Do you think I was protected from that?"

She jumped to her feet, dumping her sewing onto the floor. Rosamund rose also and faced her friend squarely. Elizabeth hurried to intervene, stepping between them.

"Victorine, hold your tongue!"

"You always take her side!" Victorine stamped her small, slipper-clad foot. "I will pull her hair if this farm girl criticizes my maman once more."

"I didn't say anything about your mother." Rosamund sighed. "But you shouldn't make my family sound like peasants."

"Bah! At least Louisiana has seceded." Victorine sniffed. "We are in this brave new Confederacy. Tennessee is still wavering."

So is Virginia, Elizabeth opened her mouth to retort, but for once, Rosamund was ahead of her, her tone firm. "Perhaps Tennesseans understand how serious a matter it is to leave the Union."

"Are you saying Orleanians are *des imbeciles*–stupid? How dare you!"

Victorine glared, and Rosamund's face flushed with emotion.

"Girls! What on earth?" Madame Corday frowned at them all from the doorway. "Are you quarreling? This isn't like you."

"It wasn't Victorine's fault," Sarah said at once, her voice shrill.

"You won't lay the blame on Rosamund," Elizabeth argued hotly, glaring at Sarah.

"That will do." Madame's tone silenced them all. "This is no time for petty bickering."

"Has something happened?" Elizabeth asked quickly.

Their headmistress's expression was somber. "I've just heard that Jefferson Davis, president of the Confederate States, has demanded the surrender of Fort Sumter."

The room became very quiet. Elizabeth could hear a bee droning from outside the window. A shaft of golden sunlight slanted through the glass pane, highlighting the polished table. All their pent-up worry and anger had suddenly vanished. The room seemed very peaceful–she had the feeling she would always remember this moment.

"What will happen now?" she whispered.

"Unless Major Anderson surrenders, I fear the talking is over," Madam Corday told them, her voice level.

"*Mon Dieu*, surely he will give in. The major is from Kentucky. I've heard he has sympathies for the South, his homeland," Victorine protested.

"I've also heard he is loyal to the oath he swore when he took up his commission," Rosamund murmured.

Her heart heavy, Elizabeth thought of Adam Cranfield, so new to his own commission, so proud of that blue uniform. And there was Stephen Hall, eager to go to war. Would his bright gold braid be tarnished with gun smoke?

For once, she was thankful for the childhood accident that had left her brother lame. At least he would not ride off to war. She drew a deep breath, trying to steady her whirling thoughts.

"Come, girls," Madame Corday said. "I'm calling everyone into the large schoolroom. We shall join together in a prayer for peace."

After Madame read aloud the Twenty-third Psalm, she led them in prayers, and Elizabeth clenched her hands together tightly. She thought of the young men in all of their military finery, of the heavy iron cannon that sat on the Battery and crowned the summit of the forts on both sides of the harbor.

"Oh, Lord, protect the soldiers, whatever the color of their uniforms."

They heard little more that afternoon. But if Sumter surrendered, Elizabeth was sure the news would have swept through the town. Everyone was on edge. Supper that night was unusually quiet, and she was not the only student to leave the food on her plate untouched.

When twilight came, Elizabeth joined Rosamund on the wide piazza. They sat side by side on a joggling board but had no heart for childish bouncing, gazing instead into the darkness. Elizabeth wished they were close enough to see the harbor. What was happening past the seawall?

"If only that silly Major Anderson hadn't moved his men to Sumter," Victorine complained from behind them. "All this fuss wouldn't have occurred."

Elizabeth thought uneasily of the night the ruse had taken place. Had she been the first to know?

"Anderson is commander of the harbor. He has the right to occupy any of the forts," Rosamund argued.

"I do believe you should be a Yankee, Rosamund," Victorine snapped.

Rosamund bit her lip and didn't answer.

The silence on the piazza was tense. Elizabeth heard the whining of a mosquito and the faint cry of a night bird. Waving the mosquito away, she tried to peer through the darkness, but all she could see were bats darting erratically across the sky.

"Time to go up to bed, girls," Madame called.

It was hard to leave the piazza, even though there was little to see. Once in bed, Elizabeth turned restlessly against the feather pillows for what seemed like hours until at last she drifted into a troubled sleep.

The trembling of her bedstead jarred her abruptly awake in the early hours of the morning. Across the room, Elizabeth heard Rosamund gasp.

Then the heavy booming came again.

Cannon fire!

## Chapter Seven

Jumping out of bed, Elizabeth pushed aside the thin summer veils of mosquito netting. She reached for a candle, but her hand shook so badly that she couldn't light it. Her heart seemed to be in her throat–she could feel it pounding.

A tiny flame sprang up on the other side of the room. Rosamund had been more successful.

Elizabeth pulled on her silk dressing gown, lit her candle from Rosamund's, and hurried into the hall. The landing was filled with girls in varying stages of undress. Where was Madame?

"What's happening? Are they shooting at us?" one of the girls called.

"We're going to die!" Sarah shrilled, her voice wobbling with hysteria.

"Stop that." Elizabeth put one hand on Sarah's shoulder and shook the younger girl gently. "Who would want to blow up a girls's school? It's the fort they're after."

Sarah pulled away. To Elizabeth's relief, the sudden glare of gaslights sprang up on the ground floor. Then she saw a circle of light slip up the wide staircase. Madame Corday, in an elegant silk robe, reached the landing and held an oil lamp high. "Now, girls," she said. "No need to panic."

"Oh, Madame! I want my mother," Sarah cried, rushing to the comforting presence of their headmistress. Madame was immediately surrounded by tearful students, all talking at once.

Elizabeth peered through the window on the landing but saw only dark tree tops. "Oh, I wish could see what was happening."

Rosamund leaned closer to whisper. "The roof. I know where we can get out onto the roof."

Elizabeth nodded in agreement. While the other girls shrieked and sobbed, Elizabeth and Rosamund padded softly down the hall toward the attic stairs.

"Wait for me." Victorine had appeared at last, her hair neatly bound up, her robe primly buttoned. But as always when she was excited, her Creole accent had thickened. "Where do we go, eh?" "We want to see the battle," Elizabeth explained. "Rosamund knows how to get to the roof."

They climbed the narrow stairs, and Rosamund showed them a large window in the front attic. "I came up weeks ago, looking for a length of material Madame wanted from her trunk."

They shoved the window sash up as far as it would go and climbed through onto the almost flat section of roof.

Creeping over the uneven shingles, the three crouched a few feet from the window and stared out over the city to the dark water beyond. Fog shrouded the shoreline. Elizabeth strained her eyes and finally made out Fort Sumter, a distant hump in the middle of the harbor.

"There!" She pointed, and the other two girls leaned forward.

Another cannon roared, and the rooftop shook faintly beneath them. Elizabeth caught her breath, hearing the high-pitched shriek, watching the red path of the shell as it curved upward, then arched and fell inside the fort.

The explosion brought tears to her eyes. There were men in the path of that deadly mortar—one of them she knew and cared about. Trembling with anxiety, she twisted a ribbon on her robe until it shredded.

Another cannon blasted, and the round shell rose through the darkness, sparks outlining its path. It looked almost like lightning, with thunder close behind, but this was man-made and even more deadly.

Had she thought war romantic? The new uniforms had looked so fine—the bands had played so merrily. Where was the music now?

As if in answer, two cannon boomed. Again, she felt the rooftop tremble.

"*Mon Dieu*, will they bring down our house?" Victorine asked in alarm. "They are brave, our Carolina troops, but they should give more thought to the town."

Around them, the houses lit up, one after another, as the sound of cannon fire roused Charleston. Soon shouts rose from the street, and Elizabeth saw clumps of men and women rushing toward the Battery, to better follow the course of the battle.

Now a whole regiment of cannon seemed to wake. Instead of single streaks of lightning, sheets of fire rent the night sky. So many shells dropped that it seemed impossible to Elizabeth that the fort would still be there. Yet, narrowing her eyes, she saw the squat brick fortress still marking the center of the harbor.

The thunder of the cannon was deafening. She saw Victorine shudder, her hands over her ears. Elizabeth found her own ears ringing. The three of them watched until rain began to fall, then scrambled back inside.

Elizabeth shivered.

"It will be daylight soon," Rosamund pointed out, staring at the cloudy sky. "Then we can see more."

"*Moi*, I'm going back to bed and never getting up," Victorine announced, her voice tremulous. "I don't want to see anything. This is horrid."

Elizabeth heard the break of a sob in her friend's voice. She gave her a quick hug. "Don't worry–the cannon won't hurt you."

Rosamund patted Victorine's shoulder, too, then the other girl hurried back to the safety of her bed.

Elizabeth entered her own room, with Rosamund behind her. It was too early to be up and about, but sleep was impossible. Elizabeth dressed hastily in the near dark, not bothering to pull on her hoops. Without them, her skirts hung limply around her ankles, but she didn't care. She did, however, take the time to reach into her trinket box for Adam's button.

"I'm going down to the kitchen," she told Rosamund, pulling a shawl over her head.

"I'll come with you." Rosamund finished braiding her fair hair and grabbed her own shawl, then followed Elizabeth out of the bedroom.

Elizabeth could hear Madame's voice at the end of the hall. By the sound, she was still occupied with comforting the younger girls.

Elizabeth and Rosamund descended the main staircase and turned to the back of the school. The kitchen was a small brick structure at the rear of the main house, to keep the heat and cooking smells out of the bigger building.

Inside the small building, they found the elderly black cook seated on a worn rush chair, sobbing lustily. Fanny pushed at the large tin kettle hung inside the big fireplace, her face drawn but composed. She looked up at them now in surprise.

"Oh, ma'am," she said. "I'm doing my best, but Annie's in such a dither."

"We'll help," Rosamund told her. "Shall I put on some porridge?"

Looking relieved, Fanny pointed them toward the pantry. When they were alone, Rosamund said in a low voice, "The wonder is that most of the slaves are so calm. Don't they know what this war could mean to them?"

*Freedom*, Elizabeth thought. Surely, they must, and yet–slaves were forbidden to learn to read and write, so they couldn't read the newspapers, and who talked politics to them?

"If they do, perhaps they're too accustomed to hiding their feelings," she whispered back. "Anyhow, Fanny is free. She's Madam's personal servant, and came with her from Britain. I don't know about the cook."

Still, it was a daunting thought. Did Hannah, who could read, hide secrets from Elizabeth? She remembered the strange adventure after Christmas. She now knew that Hannah had her own thoughts, perhaps her own plans, and they might not include Elizabeth. It made her feel strangely lonely–she and

Hannah had been so close as children. But to be fair, Elizabeth had never shared her feelings about Adam Cranfield, still abashed to admit the strength of her emotions for a man she barely knew.

They carried an armload of foodstuffs from the pantry to the kitchen. While Rosamund stirred meal into the big kettle of hot water, Elizabeth help Fanny fix pots of tea and grind coffee beans.

By the time they helped bring in trays of food, the rain had stopped and daylight was breaking over the horizon. Elizabeth ached to get back to the roof. Cannon still boomed.

Madame Corday smiled when she saw them. "Girls, thank you, Everyone will feel better with something warm inside them."

The younger girls were herded into the dining room, and Madame cajoled them into eating. Elizabeth ate a few bites of porridge and gulped down the hot tea. Then, catching Rosamund's eyes, she motioned toward the staircase.

Rosamund nodded, and they excused themselves. On the second floor they found Victorine in her bedroom doorway, fully dressed and holding a pair of gilt-embellished opera glasses. Still pale, she looked more composed.

"Fanny didn't come up. Where's our tea?"

"Downstairs. You'll have to fetch it yourself." Elizabeth smiled at her to see that Victorine had made an effort after all. "And while you have your tea, let me borrow your opera glasses."

Victorine gave them over, and Elizabeth and Rosamund ran down the hall and up the narrow attic stairs. Without her hoops, she could easily manage climbing out the window, and they soon regained their former post on the roof.

On houses nearby, other roofs were crowded with people. With her borrowed opera glasses, Elizabeth could see that the Battery itself was thronged with people—men, women, children—all staring out over the harbor.

The morning light was dim, though some of the fog had lifted. But smoke from the cannon fire drifted over the water, and Elizabeth searched once more to find the fort.

"Let me see," Rosamund said from beside her.

"In a moment. Oh, there it is." She narrowed her gaze on the fort, just as a burst of smoke and flame answered the incoming shells.

"They're firing back!" Elizabeth lowered the glasses.

Rosamund grabbed them. "Didn't you think you would?"

"Yes, but still—" Elizabeth felt a lump come into her throat. "It's really war, then."

The rooftop shuddered as another round of Charleston cannon roared. Rosamund put out one hand, and Elizabeth gripped it tightly, suddenly afraid.

They spend most of the day on the roof, anxiously watching the battle. Several times Elizabeth considered trying to sneak down to the Battery, which was crowded with spectators.

"Madame has locked the gates, and she's holding the keys herself." Rosamund had been inside to fetch them slices of bread and cheese. "She doesn't intend for any of her students to get blown up."

"I want to do something," Elizabeth raged. Her legs ached from crouching on the uneven roof, and her tired eyes stung from the bluish-brown haze. The acrid scent of smoke lingered, and it seemed hard to breathe. The air over Charleston was tainted with the fumes of battle.

"You wouldn't be able to do anything, and you've probably got a better view from here." Rosamund's tone was soothing.

Victorine came to the attic window and stared at them, but declined to climb out. "You're getting soiled from the cinders," she said. "And your hair's a mess, Elizabeth. Besides, you could be in danger, n'cest-ce pas? Please come inside."

Elizabeth didn't reply. "Look!" she said, straightening her aching legs to stand and see more clearly.

"Careful," Rosamund warned. "What is it?"

"A ship! It must be reinforcements for Fort Sumter, at last. And another, and another—three ships."

But although the ships lingered against the horizon, they made no move to come into the harbor.

"Why don't they come?" Elizabeth demanded.

"They'd get blown to bits by the shells," Rosamund guessed.

"Cowards," Elizabeth muttered beneath her breath. "Oh, look at the smoke from Fort Sumter. It's on fire again."

Thinking of Adam Cranfield fighting on top of a lighted powder keg, Elizabeth shuddered. She reached inside her apron pocket, clutching the brass button from Adam's uniform so tightly that her fingers ached. In a strange way, it made her feel closer to him in his time of danger.

Why hadn't she voiced her feelings when she'd last seen him? She cursed her stupid pride forgetting in the way. What if he died and she never saw him again? She tried to push aside the painful thoughts.

The battle raged on. Each time the fort flamed, the Yankee troops managed to put out the fire and keep their smaller cannon in action.

"They're cheering Anderson on the docks," Rosamund pointed out as the faint echoes reached them, "for continuing to fight, despite the fires."

"Whose side are they on?" Elizabeth mocked, glancing at Victorine.

Her friend seemed unfazed. "*Eh, bien*, I never said we did not appreciate courage in our enemies," she said, her voice calm. "By the by, Madame had spoken with our neighbors. She said that the reports so far of few wounded and no deaths. It only proves that God must be on our side."

Elizabeth bit back a quick retort, and Rosamund looked grave. "I cannot think that God would enjoy looking over a battlefield," she said softly.

About six, the rain fell again, driving Elizabeth inside the attic, though she refused to leave the window.

Not until Madame herself came up to the attic did Elizabeth go reluctantly to bed.

"I know I won't be able to sleep," she protested.

"Try," Madame said firmly. "We don't know how long this battle will continue."

Elizabeth pulled off her damp clothes and fell into bed. But although her head ached and her whole body felt sore, the pounding of cannon made sleep impossible. She pulled out her journal and opening it to a blank page.

*Victorine is sure that the Confederates are God's Chosen. I almost wish I were*

> *so certain, that I didn't remember that those Yankee soldiers have wives and sisters and mothers praying hard for them, too. Are wartime sermons being preaching in Boston*

*and Washington City, just as in Charleston? How do we know we are right and*

*they are wrong? And what are the slaves praying for? Victorine's eyes shine*

*when she speaks of the Southern Cause. Will her war be easier than mine, as a*

*result, or harder?*

Later, she drifted in and out of a restless slumber, waking early on Saturday morning. Where was the roar of cannon? Had Sumter fallen? Elizabeth's heart pounded.

For once, Rosamund still slept, but she stirred when Elizabeth reached for her robe. "What is it?"

"I don't know. It's so quiet."

Rosamund went to the window and pushed up the sash, despite the early-morning chill. "The wind's changed to the west. It will be harder to hear the bombardment. But the sun is shining. We'll be able to see more clearly."

Elizabeth found her slippers and hurried to the attic. Little had changed. The cannon still pounded. Fort Sumter now showed gaping holes from the shelling, but the fort's smaller cannon fired back. The Union ships still lingered outside the harbor. The Battery was still crowded with spectators. The fighting continued.

She had thought of war as one quick brilliant battle, not days of worry and noise and danger. Elizabeth sighed and went back down to dress.

She, Rosamund, and Victorine and the other girls gathered in the dining room to sip weak tea and eat corn cakes burned at the edges.

"Annie must still be in a dither," Elizabeth remarked, frowning at the blackened edge of her cornbread.

"Girls," Madame Corday said, coming into the dining room. "A neighbor has brought word that they need cartridge bags for the Dahlgren guns. If you wish, you can work on this together."

A murmur of assent rose at once, and there was a rush for the largest schoolroom. Tables were cleared of their neglected books and ink wells, and sewing baskets appeared. Madame brought out piles of worn linen, and Elizabeth chose to cut instead of sew. Ripping through the soft cloth vented some of her frustration.

They worked in silence, listening to the faint drone of guns until one of the girls, who had gone to the kitchen for more tea, ran into the room. "Fanny says she heard from the housemaid next door that Fort Sumter is afire again. They're saying in town that everyone there is going to burn up!"

Elizabeth dropped her scissors and ran for the attic. Rosamund was behind her, but Elizabeth didn't wait. Stopping only to snatch up the opera glasses from her bedroom, she climbed the next stairs and then back onto the roof.

She strained to see through the glasses, then noted a neighbor with a telescope on a nearby roof.

"What do you see?" she called.

"They're dumping barrels of gunpowder into the sea," he answered. "But the tide is out, and the barrels are still too close. Our gunners are aiming at them."

Elizabeth heard Rosamund gasp. She herself was mute from horror. If the militia fire hit the powder–

The result came even as she thought. The explosion was so huge that the rooftop shuddered beneath them, and the windowpanes rattled. Through the glasses, Elizabeth saw a burst of burning brick and timbers explode from the fort. Another explosion followed, and then another. Would anyone be left alive inside the fortress?

Elizabeth felt tears rush down her cheeks. Where was Adam in that purgatory of flame and suffocating smoke?

It was past noon when a shell shattered the flagstaff at the fort, and the Stars and Stripes fell. Elizabeth narrowed her eyes to see past the smoke. Was the Union flag up again? She thought so.

In the early afternoon the shelling slowed. Elizabeth made out a small boat rowing toward Fort Sumter. "I think they carry a small white flag."

It seemed forever until the boat returned to the Charleston docks. Turning the opera glasses toward the harbor, Elizabeth could see spectators crowding around the men who came ashore. What was the news? The echoing cheers told clearly enough.

"Sumter has surrendered," Elizabeth said aloud. She looked at Rosamund, and they clasped hands briefly. Inside the attic, Victorine danced with joy.

Stephen Hall would be ecstatic. Back home in Virginia, her father would cheer, also. What Elizabeth felt, she wasn't certain. She didn't mean to betray the cause sacred to her family and friends, yet how could it be wrong to pray for Adam Cranfield's safety. And what about all the slaves who longed for freedom?

She twisted the button inside her pocket again, her emotion as confused as the babel of sound that rose to the rooftops.

Sunday, the church bells rang throughout the day in noisy celebration. With the cannon -quieted at last, Madame released her students from the school grounds. In the afternoon Elizabeth, Rosamund and Victorine walked down to the Battery. On the way, Elizabeth made a quick side trip to check on Hannah.

She seemed calm but subdued. Her dark-complected oval face was curiously blank when Elizabeth told her how happy she was to see her safe.

"I was in no danger," Hannah said. "Not from the cannon fire, at least."

Elizabeth stared at her old companion, wishing she did not, these days, hear overtones of meaning in their conversation that she had never guessed at before. "What do you mean?"

"Nothing." Hannah sighed. "South Carolina has won, again."

"Did you think Sumter would be able to hold out?"

"I expected more of Mr. Lincoln," Hannah said quietly.

Startled, Elizabeth protested, "What do you know of the Northern president?"

"I read one of his speeches," Hannah murmured.

More questions rushed into Elizabeth's mind. She wasn't sure she wanted to know the answers.

"Come along, Elizabeth," Victorine called from the front of the dressmaker's shop, where she and Rosamund had lingered to examine the fine silks and satins.

"In a moment," Elizabeth answered. In a lower voice, she said to Hannah, "You haven't been out at night again, have you?" She gazed hard at her friend's face.

"No, Miss Elizabeth." But Hannah did not meet her eye.

With that, Elizabeth had to be content. She left feeling more confused than ever. The whole world was changing, and with it every part of her life. She felt as if she stood on shifting sand.

She was silent as they strode along, while Rosamund and Victorine chatted about being thankful for the lovely quiet after the cannon's clamor and the warm sunshine after the haze of gun smoke. At the harbor, Charleston citizens crowded the seaside, laughing and cheering. Flags draped the buildings.

Elizabeth stared out at the ruined fort and couldn't join the gaiety.

"Miss Elizabeth, there you are. I've been looking all over. They told me at the school you'd be here." Stephen Hall's impetuous embrace left Elizabeth flushed and startled

"Are you well?" She stared at him. He needed a shave, and his uniform showed a tiny rip on the sleeve. Otherwise, he looked hardly the worse for wear.

"Shoot." Stephen grinned. "Their cannon fire didn't get close to us, hardly. Their guns were too light, you see, for the range. I had a splinter from a shell tear my sleeve, that's all. Isn't it a grand victory?"

"Grand," Elizabeth echoed. "But what about the Union forces?"

"They'll be marching the Yankees out soon. They're shipping them back to New York, and good riddance." Stephen fingered the rip in his uniform, frowning at its imperfection.

Elizabeth braced herself. "Were there many killed?"

"That's the wonder of it," Stephen told her. "Not a one, despite the fires and the shelling. Anderson wouldn't use his heavy guns, you see, because they were so exposed. He must have figured it would make no difference in the long run–he was so obviously outmatched."

"Bless him," Elizabeth murmured, feeling a great weight lift. And yet—

She stared out to sea and noticed a handful of small boats. Spectators were hurrying to inspect the site of the battle for themselves, even before the combatants had been evacuated.

"My commander's wife is throwing a celebration party." Stephen reached for her hand. "She's sending a note to Madame Corday. Will you come?"

"I suppose," Elizabeth answered, her mind elsewhere. "Could you get us a boat?"

"Now?" He sounded surprised.

"Yes, I want to see the fort when the troops leave," Elizabeth told him. Until she saw Adam Cranfield with her own eyes, she could not be convinced of his safely.

"You're right—it would be a lark," he agreed. "I'll see what I can do. Wait here."

Elizabeth nodded as he walked closer to the harbor. Rosamund bent closer to whisper, "What are you up to now?"

"I want to go, *aussi*," Victorine called. "What fun, eh?"

Elizabeth didn't feel the surrender would be fun, but she had to see. They waited until Stephen ran back to find them.

"I must have hired the last boat in the harbor," he boasted, "and at an exorbitant rate, I'll say. But anything for my lady."

Elizabeth's thanks were fervent. She pushed back a wave of guilt. Stephen would enjoy the closer view, and his allowance from his wealthy father was generous. Still, she found it hard to meet his gaze when he helped her into the small rowboat.

Once the boatman pushed them off, Stephen bent to the oars and had no more breath for conversation. As they crossed the water, Elizabeth stared at the gaps in Fort Sumter's blackened walls and wondered once more than anyone had come out alive.

When they neared the fort, Stephen lifted his oars from the water. As the boat drifted, they all gazed at the troops marching out to the docks, a faint tune in the background. Elizabeth felt her eyes moisten. The Union soldiers were marching out to the strains of "Yankee Doodle."

Elizabeth lifted the opera glasses she had brought along and stared hard at the men marching silently out of the ruined fort. Because they were stained with smoke and grime from the battle, it was hard to distinguish faces. Yet she was sure she would know one man if she could just find him.

There! Gasping, she narrowed her eyes. There was Adam, his face blackened with smoke, one side of his dark hair singed away, an angry red burn across his cheek. He looked drawn and weary, and he marched stiffly. But he walked off the island on his own two feet. He was alive and whole.

"Thank God," Elizabeth whispered, wishing she could reach out across the salt water and bridge the gap between them. It was a gap of more than water and rock and sand. The war had begun now. There was no going back. He was a Yankee lieutenant who would certainly recover and fight again. She was a daughter of Virginia, and every tie of family and friends and upbringing showed her that her loyalty was to her state. There was no chance of any emotion between them, despite her memories of a heart-stopping waltz, a passionate kiss on a dark beach. It was over. Her duty and surely her heart belonged here.

Stephen reached for her hand. "It will be a grand celebration. Are you proud of me, Elizabeth?"

She forced herself to smile. "Of course."

He gripped her hand tightly. Elizabeth fought the need to look back at the Union troops now loaded onto the ferry, and the man going out of her life forever. Oh, Adam!

A bright flame had burned briefly, but the winds of change had snuffed it out too soon. The pain she felt at its absence—was this the first casualty of war?

## Chapter Eight

"We're on our way to stomp those Yankees, boys!" the young man in the gray uniform yelled from the front of the train car.

"Whoo-ee! You got that right." Rousing cheers from the other men answered him.

Jolted by the moving train, Elizabeth gripped the seat as she looked around her. The car was crowded with colorful uniforms as young Southerners hastened to join the troops gathering in Virginia, now that the Old Dominion had formally seceded.

She saw wealthy young men from Virginia's tidewater plantations dressed in elaborate tailor-made uniforms–they reminded her of Stephen. Some had slaves along to handle their baggage. Those elegant young officers rode side by side with buckskin-clad mountaineers from the hill country. All seemed eager for a fight.

Trying to ease her tired back, Elizabeth shifted in her seat. She looked through the window toward the Virginia countryside, so lush and green it made her feel refreshed, despite her long ride. She brushed her lap free of the cinders flying back from the steam engine, wishing she could send the young soldiers back where they belonged, to studying their schoolbooks or cobbling shoes or plowing their fields.

After Sumter's fall, she had hoped briefly that this almost bloodless victory would end the conflict. The North would know the secessionists meant business. The South would have satisfied its honor. Instead, Sumter seemed only the beginning. In the two months after the fort had fallen, Arkansas, North Carolina, and Tennessee, as well as Virginia, had seceded to join the Confederate Cause; President Lincoln had asked for Northern volunteers to bolster the small regular army, and Britain's Queen Victoria had dashed Southerners' hopes of international support by announcing that her country would remain neutral.

Bored with sitting, Elizabeth reached down to open the carpetbag at her feet. She pulled out her journal and a pencil, but the bouncing of the train car made writing impossible. Sighing, she chewed on her pencil's end and reread an April entry,

*Since Sumter's fall, everyone in Charleston celebrated for days, with victory*

*parties and parades. I want to be happy, to dance with Stephen and share his*

*joy. But I can't help thinking of Adam, his pain at the Yankee defeat, dangers*

*he may yet face in battle. Where is he now?*

*Everyone thinks the war ended with Sumter, but not Madame Corday.*

*She sat us down today with strips of clean linen and a book of physiology, saying,*

*"I'm going to show you how to bind wounds and render aid."*

*"But we won the battle," Victorine protested.*

*"The war is just beginning," Madame told us. "My husband was a British officer in the Crimean War, and later in India, where he was*

*killed. I learned these lessons the hard way, girls. It doesn't hurt to be*

*prepared."*

*So, despite Victorine's delicate stomach, Madame led us through a lesson on broken bones and fever, tourniquets and wrapping of gunshot*

*wounds. Perhaps because of her experience on her family's farm, Rosamund*

*listened quietly, but it made my stomach turn at some of the pictures in*

*the book.*

Gripping the journal firmly, Elizabeth made another attempt. Scribbling hard, she wrote:

*I miss Hannah. But she wished to stay in Charleston for the summer.*

Elizabeth remembered their parting.

"My work at the modiste's is more interesting than churning butter or ironing clothes back at the plantation," Hannah had said.

"Is that all?" Elizabeth was finally brave enough to ask. "Or is it your nighttime activities—is that why you stay, Hannah?"

Hannah had hesitated.

"I don't want you to get hurt," Elizabeth told her. "If you're doing something illegal, something dangerous—"

Hannah bit her lip. "Your brother says we all have to live with our conscience.

That's the final law."

"But—"

"And my mama told me always to stand tall!" Her eyes flashed. Elizabeth hadn't tried to argue any more.

*God keep her safe*, she wrote now.

The car bounced even harder. Her pencil point broke, and she almost dropped her journal. Then the train slowed, with a series of jerks and shrieking of brakes, and she saw the Richmond station approaching. She hurried to put her book back into her bag, eager to step down from the train.

When ancient Uncle Elijah met her at the station, his grin wide against his dark skin, she felt as if she was already home.

"Welcome back, Miz Elizabeth," he said in the Virginia drawl that sounded so good to her ears.

"I'm so glad to be home," she told him, smiling and handing him a small parcel. "I brought you some bonbons from Charleston. Just don't let my father see them."

His grin revealed several missing teeth, the price he'd paid for his love of sweets. "Thank you, Miz Elizabeth. Got to get your trunks to the carriage, or the Master will say we been too slow."

He hurried to load her luggage, and Elizabeth followed more slowly. Her father–the only part of her homecoming she did not relish.

"Ready, Miz Lizabeth?" Elijah called.

She allowed him to hand her up into the open carriage. The ride back to the Stafford plantation, River Run, seemed all too brief. They passed fields of tobacco, with black field hands bent double as they set out the young plants under an overseer's watchful gaze. The sun was warm, and Elizabeth opened her parasol. The men had no shade.

Feeling guilty, she looked ahead and watched the steady trotting of the horses pulling the carriage. She was glad for the slight breeze that ruffled her hair beneath her stylish bonnet. The gentle rhythm of the horses' hooves was soothing.

Why did she see everything differently these days? There were new awarenesses she was never able to forget–the tragedy of the slave mart, the shock of Hannah's deliberate absence, the realization that Hannah had her own mind. The Elizabeth who returned home after her first year at school had changed more than she–more than anyone–would ever have expected.

As the carriage turned into the long drive that led up to the handsome porticoed mansion, she saw rosebushes heavy with buds. The air smelled fresh and clean after the cinders and smoke of the train ride, and Elizabeth felt her spirits rise again.

Her favorite gelding would be waiting in the stables, ready for long rides along the river. She was home!

When the carriage stopped in front of the house, the big doors opened. Her brother, John, limped down the wide steps, his descent slow and awkward.

Elizabeth hurried to meet him. "John, how are you?"

He gripped her hands briefly, his somber expression lightening behind the wire spectacles. "You're looking very well, Elizabeth. I know you enjoyed Charleston, although your letters were brief. As for the school, did they turn you into a Bluestocking, yet?"

She laughed at his mild teasing. "Not quite. I'll never be the scholar that you are. But it was much better than I feared. I thought I'd be bored, but Madame has so many interesting stories and some really good books, too, John."

It was his turn to chuckle. "I'm glad you've discovered that, at last," he said. "How is Hannah?"

"She's well and enjoying her new employment."

"Good." He looked away from her gaze. "I feel a bit responsible, you see."

They walked slowly up the wide steps, Elizabeth dawdling to accommodate John's hesitate gait, the result of a childish riding accident.

As they entered the front hall a door banged shut. Elizabeth bracd herself. Footsteps echoed, then William Stafford's broad, stocky frame seemed to dominate the hallway.

"You look vigorous and red-cheeked, Elizabeth. A smooth journey?" He gave her a brief kiss on the cheek, then stepped back to look her up and down.

"Yes, sir," she answered, fighting the impulse to stand up straighter, like a soldier under review.

"And how was school? A fine lady now, are we?"

"I don't know about that, sir, but I've truly learned a great deal. The books we read—" "Good. We'll hear all about it at dinner. Mr and Mrs. Amhurst will be here with their daughter. A little party for you."

"How nice," Elizabeth said formally. "This was a welcome-home treat for her? If so, her father might have noticed that she detested Missy Amhurst, a slight girl without an original thought in her head. Or had Missy really been invited for John's benefit. Elizabeth glanced at her brother, whose expression was blank.

"You'll want to unpack and rest after your journey," William Stafford said. "John, have you finished those accounts?"

"Yes, sir," John said at once.

"Bring them into my study, then. And ring for some more port."

She never seemed important enough to hold her father's attention for long. As the two men turned down the hall, Elizabeth gathered her skirts to climb the wide staircase to her old bedroom. It felt empty, somehow, without Hannah. She missed her childhood companion.

Elizabeth removed her traveling bonnet and washed the railway soot from her hands and face. Then she made her way down the back stairs, the better to evade her father, and headed for the stables.

The familiar smell of horses, hay, and manure met her at the wide doors. Elizabeth smiled at the earthy fragrance. This at least was the same. She said hello to the stable hand and hurried to the last stall, eager to see her favorite.

But a small, dun-colored mare occupied the stall. Elizabeth turned in shock.

"Andrew! Where is Smoke? He's not been ill?"

The slight black man looked down at the straw-covered brick floor, as if not wanting to meet her gaze. "H's not here, Miz Lizbet. The Master done traded him."

"What? That was my horse! How could he do that?" Elizabeth felt her face flush as outrage swept through her, closing her throat and making her chest ache.

His nervousness evident, the stable hand chewed his lip. "Smoke went lame, Miz Lizbet. I reckoned he'd recover, in time, but the Master said best be rid of a bad bargain."

Elizabeth clenched her hands so tightly at her sides that her nails cut into her palms. She forced her hands open, trying to control her rage.

"I's sorry, Miss." He still stared at the ground.

"It's not your fault. Thank you, Andrew."

But when she turned back toward the house, she was almost running. She had loved that horse! Smoke had been her father's gift to her, the most special gift she'd ever received. The gelding had been her pet, and her father knew it.

Inside, she swept down the hall and entered the study without knocking.

William Stafford looked up in surprise. After one glance at her face, John seemed tactfully absorbed in a pile of papers on the side table.

"How could you trade Smoke?" Too angry to be tactful, Elizabeth stood in front of the big desk.

"Elizabeth, I though you went away to learn to behave like a lady. Modulate your tone, if you please." William Stafford narrowed his gaze–he had eyes like a hawk, she had often thought as a child.

Elizabeth wanted to scream. "Why did you trade my favorite horse?"

"He went lame in his right rear fetlock, Elizabeth. We have no room in the stable for a cripple."

She thought she saw, from the corner of her eye, her brother wince. "Smoke was my horse, and I loved him! You should have waited to consult me."

"I'm in charge of this plantation and every person and beast on it, as you well know, Elizabeth Margaret Stafford." William Stafford drummed his fingers impatiently on the polished walnut of his desktop. " The horse couldn't be ridden, couldn't be used for breeding. I made the only rational decision. It isn't proper for you to question my judgment. I provided another mount for you, a well-trained and healthy young mare. You should thank me, instead of indulging in sentimental female tantrums."

"And I have no say in choosing which horse I ride? My feelings mean nothing?" Elizabeth felt rigid with rage.

"This is foolishness, Elizabeth. I have work to do. You'd better change for dinner. Our guests will be arriving soon."

As usual, there was no discussion allowed. The king had made his decree. Elizabeth fought to control her temper, to hold back the rush of angry words that would only make the situation worse. Trembling, she left the room as impetuously as she had entered.

She ran up the steps, forgetting to lift her long skirts and stumbling once on her hem, almost falling. She slammed the bedroom door, and in the privacy of her room, threw herself onto the bed, angry tears escaping her control at last. Sobbing, she beat the pillows until a stray feather or two escaped to float on the warm, still air.

"I loved that horse. Smoke was mine. How can he be so unfeeling?" There was no answer, no one on the plantation to take her side. How could she endure a whole summer of her father's domination? Elizabeth had barely been home an hour, and already she felt suffocated.

Sobbing until she was exhausted, Elizabeth fell into an uneasy sleep. When she woke, the line of sunlight against the wall had shifted, and she could tell from the fading light that much of the day had passed. She had to change. Jumping up, she went to her bureau and glanced into the looking glass on the wall. Her face was marked by the folds of the pillow, her eyes puffy, her hair in wild disarray. What did it matter?

She forced herself to wash her face and comb her hair. The water in the pitcher was tepid, but she had no time to ring for more. Besides, if her father heard her ask, he might punish the household slaves for the omission, and they suffered enough from his tyranny.

No wonder Hannah had not wanted to return to the plantation. What slave would? Having your life arranged for you, never having your wishes consulted, what kind of life was that? Elizabeth looked out the windows, from the stable with its missing horse to the slave cabins beyond. How had she ever believed slavery to be a benevolent system? How blind she had been.

The thought kept her silent as Josie, one of the house servants, came in to help her dress in a pale green gown trimmed with gold ribbon and white rosettes. Elijah had put her trunks into her room earlier, and Elizabeth opened the smaller one, finding the hair bow Hannah had made her for Christmas. It made her feel closer to her missing friend as she pinned it into her upswept hair.

By the time she came slowly down the winding staircase, she could hear the chatter of new voices in the hall. The Amhursts had arrived.

"Miss Elizabeth, don't you look fine. Charleston has agreed with you, I see," Mr. Amhurst told her.

"Thank you, sir. How nice to see you again." Elizabeth accepted Mrs. Amhurst's peck on her cheek. The matron was bosomy and her fading blonde hair was adorned with gold ribbons and pricy ostrich feathers.

"You must tell us all about the latest fashions in the city," Mrs. Amhurst gushed. Her daughter, a paler copy of her mother, nodded.

The bustle of greetings covered the awkwardness of facing her father again. But William Stafford seemed aware of no strain as he waved them all into the parlor. Why should he, Elizabeth thought bitterly. He is accustomed to having everyone bow to his command.

Elizabeth sat on a brocaded sofa with the Virginia ladies and recounted all the millinery details she could think of, then forced herself to smile civilly as she listened to a lengthy account of the Amhurst's flower garden.

"The lilacs were so pale this year, although I had the slaves move them to the other side of the garden to get more sun. . ."

Elizabeth was relieved when the black butler called them in to dinner. Seated between John and Mr. Amhurst, she could taste her cold consume and listen to the men discuss the latest rumors of war. Josie and another house slave, Charles, served the food silently and efficiently.

"Alexandria has been occupied by Union troops," Mr. Amhurst told the other diners. "So close to Washington City, it's hardly a surprise. But the use of force has mobilized much of the state.

"Now that Richmond has been made the capital of the Confederacy, Virginia is sure to take a leading role in the conflict. We have troops at Fairfax Station, Centreville, and a good number at Manassas Station. Troops are arriving from South Carolina, I hear."

"Virginia's young men are rushing to sign up," Mrs. Amhurst added. "Dear lads."

William Stafford nodded. "John will leave any day now."

Elizabeth gasped. Her brother, who couldn't march a mile, hated guns, and could hardly sit a horse after his childhood riding accident, was to be a soldier?

"Surely not," she exclaimed. "John's reading for the bar." She couldn't point out her brother's physical disabilities. "What about his law studies?"

Her father waved his hand in dismissal. "All that can wait. Nothing supersedes the needs of our state. Did the men of Virginia hold back during the *first* American Revolution? We must act as bravely."

"I trust you will never have cause to doubt my courage, sir." John's voice was quiet but firm.

Elizabeth swallowed hard. No one had ever called her brother a coward, despite his retiring nature. She had heard John deal competently with plantation business and argue calmly but sternly with their overseer. It was only their hardheaded father who made him look pale by comparison.

Mrs. Amhurst seemed not to notice the tension around the dinner table. She accepted another muffin as Josie held out the silver tray. "We've all been sewing for the Cause," she told Elizabeth while sipping her wine. "You must join us, dear. The church is filled with borrowed sewing machines, and we all do our part. With her own hands, Missy has already sewn three shirts for the soldiers."

'How commendable." Elizabeth smiled at the other girl, but she kept her tone neutral. She hated needlework. What a choice. She could spend her summer wrangling with her father or closeted with Mrs. Amhurst and her colorless daughter. To be fair, the ladies of the neighborhood were certainly not all so empty-headed, but the mood of the sewing party was still not likely to lift her own troubled spirits.

"Have you learned any new stitches at school, Elizabeth?" Missy Amhurst asked timidly from her seat on John's other side. Her father was definitely playing match-maker, but Elizabeth doubted that John could be swayed on such an important decision.

With some effort, Elizabeth kept her tone even. "Actually, we've discussed Charles Darwin's theories on the origin of species by natural selection. We've read Mr. Dicken's latest novel and examined social conditions in industrial cities. We've studied history and philosophy and the theory of mathematics."

They all stared at her. Missy looked bewildered, and Elizabeth's father was frowning.

"That's not why I sent you off to school, young lady, to get peculiar ideas put into your head."

Elizabeth pressed her lips together, wondering if she has gone too far. Her father was perfectly capable of refusing to send her back to Madame Corday's Academy. The thought of not returning to her friends, to Madame's comforting affection, sent a pang of alarm through her.

"You must allow Elizabeth her little jest, sir," John said.

Elizabeth felt warmed by this show of support. "Yes, forgive me," she spoke quickly. "Missy, I've learned several fancy stitches that might interest you. I'll show you in the parlor after dinner." Missy smiled, and her father returned his attention to his roasted duck. Elizabeth drew a deep breath, vowing to keep closer guard on her unruly tongue. She hoped she could remember the intricate needlework patterns. She had seen Victorine busy with her needle often enough.

"Did you see much of the Battle of Fort Sumter, Elizabeth?" Mr. Amhurst asked. "That galvanized our state to action more effectively than any argument on states' rights. It must have been most exciting."

Her appetite fading, Elizabeth pushed the peas on her plate around with her fork. "Madame did not allow us out of the school grounds."

She looked up to see her father nod his approval and was belatedly thankful for Madame's caution. "But we heard the roar of cannon. The house shook for days. And we saw the smoke from the fort when it was set afire."

"We saw General Lee at church while we were in Richmond," Mrs. Amhurst said. "Such an elegant officer, though grayer than I remembered. You know that rascal Lincoln offered him the command of the whole Union army? But Lee declined, noble man, saying he could not raise his hand against his own relatives, and he resigned his commission."

The talk turned to more preparations of war. Elizabeth's thoughts wandered.

After dinner, the women retired to the parlor, to be joined eventually by the men, who had lingered over port and cigars. Elizabeth retrieved an old sewing basket and managed to satisfy Missy's curiosity about fancy patterns. She was thankful when the evening ended. After saying good night, she escaped to her own bed chamber.

She allowed Josie to undo the hooks and eyes that closed the back of her bodice, then sent her off to bed. Unbuttoning her waistband, Elizabeth realized how much she missed Victorine's merry laugh and Rosamund's cheerful company. Hannah wasn't here, either, to exchange secret grumbling about Elizabeth's father. John might share his sister's frustration, but he was too cautious to vent his feelings aloud. Sighing, Elizabeth pulled on her nightdress.

Before she climbed into bed, she opened her trinket box and found her brass button from Adam's uniform. Pressing it to her cheek for a moment, she pulled out her journal.

*Despite his angry words, Adam has changed my life, touching both my*
   *heart and my mind. I can never look at a slave again and be blind to*
      *this great injustice.*

The day passed with little excitement, save for another explosion from their father. His face set grimly, John had indeed ridden into Richmond to sign up–and had come promptly home again to say that he had been turned down—for obvious reasons.

"They offered me a post as a recruiting officer" John told their father.

"A fine place for my son to be, sitting on his rear in a recruiting office." His face flushed, William Stafford paced up and down in his study. "The Staffords deserve better treatment. I have friends in the state government. They'll be hearing from me."

For her part, Elizabeth was relieved. She already had enough young men in uniform to worry about.

Letters came from Victorine and from Madame Corday and from Rosamund, home in Tennessee.

Victorine wrote:

*Charleston is still very festive. The latest step is the Secession Two-Step. I*

*wish Papa would allow me to come home for the summer, but he fears*
*New Orleans' Yellow Fever.*

Madame wrote of a concert and a new seaport and mentioned an interesting essay.

Rosamund's letter said:

*My brothers had a terrible argument over Tennessee joining the Confederacy.*
*Daniel says it is not right to break up our nation. Thomas swears the original*
*compact of states allowed for secession and feels we must support our state.*
*I am greatly troubled. I do not know where this family discord will lead. I miss*
*everyone at school, and especially you, Elizabeth. God keep you and your*
*family safe.*

The prayer seemed bitter comfort, as their father worked hard to get John a commission in the Southern forces. But even his fox-hunting cronies could not be convinced of John's stamina.

It was another letter that broke the impasse. Working in the rose garden, Elizabeth saw a brown horse come up the drive. Its rider was Mr. Amhurst again. He hailed her cheerfully. "I have a letter for you, Miss Elizabeth."

Dusting her apron, she stood up. "A letter?"

"One of Mary's nieces has come out of Washington City, and she brought the letter with her. "Tis from your cousin who married that Yankee fellow."

"Lucy! Oh, thank you." Elizabeth smiled. "I haven't heard from her in ages."

She took the guest inside, saw him welcomed into her father's study, then stepped aside and ripped open the missive.

*Elizabeth, my dear, I've missed you. Can you come for a visit?*
*Nathan*

*must go to New York on business, and my mother cannot come.
Her health is*

*poor. We are expecting an addition to our family by Christmas time, and*

*Nathan fears to leave me alone. He thinks I will pine away!*

Lucy was having a baby! She was scarcely older than Elizabeth. But this was a chance to see her cousin again, to see Washington City, and just as compelling, to get away from her father! Elizabeth's spirits leaped at the thought.

She finished the letter quickly.

*I have obtained passes for you and John—no one will suspect him of being a*

*combatant. There are some advantages to marrying a Yankee,* Lucy concluded

tartly. *I do hope you can come.*

Mr. Amhurst stayed for dinner, and Elizabeth waited until he took his leave before facing her father. As she had feared, he frowned down at her.

"Waltz off into Yankee-controlled territory? Of course not."

"But, sir, Lucy has obtained a pass for John, he can take me to her. What dangers would there be? No armies are engaged."

William Stafford's expression became thoughtful. "Into Washington itself, eh? You could get a good look around, John. Report back to our commanders here. The South has friends in Washington already, but more information can hardly hurt. Perhaps this will give you something significant to do for the Cause, after all."

Elizabeth was careful not to smile. She would use any excuse her father offered.

"I shall go to the courthouse and see about getting you both passes through our lines." William Stafford poured himself another glass of port, staring into its ruby depths.

Elizabeth shared an exultant glance with her brother. Freedom!

## Chapter Nine

"Where's your pass?" The Yankee sentry demanded, his tone rude. "And what business have you here?"

While John argued their case, Elizabeth pulled her cloak closer. The rain blew inside the carriage with every gust of wind. She wrinkled her nose at the smells of garbage lying in the muddy strets of Washington City, wishing she could be done with the nervous sentries who stood guard at every major thoroughfare.

She thought, you'd think this town was already besieged.

This sentry finally let them pass. "But you must be on your way within a sennight," he told John sternly.

Elizabeth shook her head. Only a week? Perhaps Lucy could find a way to extend their visit.

Troops crowded the streets and stations as they had in Charleston, but these men spoke with different accents. John quietly pointed out the clipped sounds of New England, which reminded Elizabeth painfully of Adam Cranfield, the broader vowels of newly recruited Midwest farm boys, and occasionally the foreign accent of a recent immigrant.

During the last part of the drive, John had explained the capital's perilous position. The ten-square-mile District of Columbia was bordered across the Potomac River by Virginia, already part of the Confederacy, and on the other side by Maryland, which had hovered on the brink of secession until Union troops moved into Baltimore in May. No wonder that the federal forces were edgy.

When they reached Lucy's small, neat home in Georgetown, Elizabeth hurried in out of the drizzling rain, while John drove their carriage around to the back.

"My dear, I am so happy to see you." Lucy hugged Elizabeth, wet cloak and all. "Was the journey disagreeable? There are soldiers everywhere these days."

"John has already been told that he must be gone within the week," Elizabeth told her cousin. "Even with the passes, we often had to argue with the guards. With every stop, you became weaker and weaker, my poor sick relative."

Lucy laughed merrily. Short and slender, she was the picture of health. Only a slightly expanded waistband betrayed her condition. "I shall remember to play the part. Come in and take off those wet things."

A hot cup of tea was very welcome after their damp ride, and Lucy had a fresh-baked cake to slice. Her elderly maid servant brought out cold meats. John soon joined them. "I've put the horses into your stables, Lucy, and thrown a tarpaulin over the carriage."

"Good. Our gentle old nag will be glad of some company," their hostess told him. "Here, we have a cup ready for you. I do thank you for bringing Elizabeth to me. I've been so lonely."

"I was happy to do it," John answered. He and Elizabeth exchanged a glance. They had agreed to say nothing of John's supposed 'spy' mission. It seemed unfair to place Lucy in an uncomfortable position. They spent the evening chatting and catching up.

By the next morning, the rain had stopped and Lucy insisted on showing them the sights.

"We must forget this troublesome war," she told them. "I want you to enjoy your visit."

As they drove through town, Elizabeth found the capital not all that impressive. True, there were stately public buildings, some still under construction, and handsome homes, but past those, shanty towns had been hastily thrown up by poorer citizens. Farther along, they saw open fields, green and marshy and occasionally dotted with cattle grazing.

The war proved impossible to ignore. As they circled back, Lucy noted, "There are extra soldiers standing guard in front of the White House."

In addition, the handsome, porticoed Treasury Building had Union troops garrisoned inside. The Capitol itself was attractive, but as of now, the new dome was incomplete, and it also had troops quartered within it.

"But President Lincoln has instructed the building to go ahead," Lucy told them. "It's a sign of his faith that the Union will continue."

Thinking of the South's wartime fervor, Elizabeth shook her head. If both sides were equally determined, how could this war end quickly?

"Have you seen him–Lincoln, I mean?" she asked her cousin. "In the South, they call him the ugliest man in the world, and devilish, to boot."

"Well, he is homely," Lucy said slowly. "Yet, not in a disagreeable way. He's tall and somewhat awkward in his movements. He wears a rusty old black frock coat, and his black hair usually needs brushing. But his eyes are wise and kind. He's friendly and yet has a strange dignity. He believes very strongly that the Union must not be destroyed, I know that."

Elizabeth tried to picture the U.S. president, whose caricatures she had seen in the *Charleston Mercury*. She'd heard so many Southerners curse Lincoln for opposing states' rights, for daring to limit the slave territories. Lucy's impression of this much-talked-about man was not what she'd expected.

Their horses struggled to pull the carriage through the sticky mud, and on a rare paved street the carriage jolted over wide cracks.

"It's the cannon," Lucy explained. "They use teams of oxen to pull the heavy artillery into place, and it ruins the streets."

"Are they so frightened of their Southern foes?" Elizabeth asked, feeling secretly gratified.

"Their fear is not unfounded," Lucy explained. "Southern sympathizers wrecked the rail lines in Maryland. But the Union forces rebuilt them. And now that the Eighth Massachusetts and the Seventh New York, said to be a crack troop, have arrived in town, the citizens of Washington are breathing easier. Even Lincoln is smiling more, they say."

Elizabeth's gaze wandered to the troops thronging the streets, drilling in open squares, or standing at attention in front of public buildings. Hundreds, thousands of Union soldiers occupied Washington.

Every time she saw a blue uniform on a tall, dark-haired man, her heart leaped, and she struggled to control her expression. Lucy seemed too busy playing tour guide to notice, but Elizabeth saw her brother glance at her curiously.

Elizabeth bit her lip. Adam Cranfield could have been sent anywhere in the Northern states. Yet there were so many Union soldiers scattered around the city, he *might* be here.

When they returned to Lucy's home, Elizabeth felt a curious disappointment. "You're being a ninny," she scolded herself under her breath. "You have no business searching for a Yankee."

Yet no one had ever affected her this way before. Adam was impossible to forget.

The next day it rained again, and she and Lucy stayed inside, snug in Lucy's small parlor. Elizabeth wished she could have gone with John—was he collecting information on troop movements, as their father had requested? Lucy assumed he had college friends to visit.

"How does it feel to marry and leave home?" Elizabeth asked her cousin, who was contentedly sewing small baby garments. "Have you any regrets about moving north?"

"I miss my family," Lucy admitted, biting off a piece of thread. "I miss you. But many Virginians have married outside the state—it's not so rare. My Nathan is a sweetheart, and he loves me dearly. I would do it again."

"And your politics—are you a Northerner already?" Elizabeth handed over the pair of scissors that Lucy had dropped.

"It would be disagreeable to argue with Nathan," Lucy admitted. "We were always taught that the husband made the decisions for the family, you know. It's not as if women can vote, after all. Does anyone except our own family care what we think about politics?"

Elizabeth frowned. "Madame Corday says women have logical brains and were meant to use them as wisely as they use their other skills."

Lucy raised her brows. "And your father sent you to *her* school?"

"I think he was more interested in her eminent family background than her philosophy of teaching," Elizabeth admitted, smiling. "But after listening to Madame, I feel I should have my own opinion. Has the South made the right choice? I've begun to believe—" she thought of the slave mart and suppressed a shiver–"that slavery is wrong. Should it be allowed to continue, just because the system makes it easier to grow crops like cotton and rice?"

"Nathan has said much the same. Yet I wonder about the landowners. Do they just give up their plantations? And what would happen to the slaves–they'd starve. What use is freedom without jobs or homes?"

"But it isn't right, Lucy!" Elizabeth paced up and down the small parlor, trying to explain. "How would you feel being sold on an auction block?"

Lucy looked shocked. "But I wouldn't be."

"If your skin was a darker shade—"

"But they're not the same as us." Lucy dropped her thimble in her agitation. "I don't wish them harm, Elizabeth, but my father always said the slaves are like children. They have to be guided, protected."

"And whipped?" Elizabeth knelt by her cousin's side. "Lucy, I saw a mother weeping when they took away her child. I've seen a man bleeding from the lash. His blood was the same color as mine."

Lucy's expression was still perplexed. She patted Elizabeth's hand. "Elizabeth, my dear. Don't worry about things you cannot change. That's what men are for, bless their sturdy hearts. John is enough of a worrier; you don't need another in the family."

"What makes you say that?" Elizabeth sat down again. Nothing she said seemed to make a dent in Lucy's way of thinking.

"He used to talk about such things, too, especially after he went North to college. And dashing around at night on mysterious errands–I did worry about him."

Her quiet scholarly brother? Talking was one thing, mysterious missions another. Elizabeth narrowed her eyes. "How did you know?"

"I didn't ask," Lucy said quickly. "Only because he had to borrow my carriage once late at night, and he didn't want my father to find out, so I covered for him. And I don't want to know what he was up to. I'm sure it was simply a boy's lark."

But Lucy threaded her needle with extra care, not meeting Elizabeth's eyes. Elizabeth's thoughts raced. What had he done on those dark nights?

She waited with increased anxiety for John to return, but the afternoon stretched into evening, and they were forced to eat a much-delayed meal without him. Lucy's house maid washed up the dishes while Lucy and Elizabeth went to the parlor for a last cup of tea.

Lucy looked puzzled and slightly annoyed. "If he decided to stay overnight with his friends, he should have sent us word."

"Men can be so thoughtless," Elizabeth agreed.

"Dear me, yes. Did I tell you how Nathan forgot his own aunt's dinner party?" Lucy began a long story about her absent husband. Elizabeth nodded and pretended to listen, but her fears for her brother grew. Was John in danger?

When they went up to bed, she was so taut with worry that her shoulders ached. She lay awake most of the night, picturing John shot by a jittery sentry, John in a spy's prison. When the dark sky lightened just before dawn, Elizabeth made up her mind. She dressed very quietly and tiptoed down the staircase. Wincing as a loose board squeaked, she held her breath. But no sleepy inquiry came from Lucy's bedroom.

Elizabeth slipped outside and around to the stable. When she opened the stable door, she was greeted by a whinny and the usual stable smells. Speaking gently to Lucy's mild-natured nag, she reached for the driving harness.

Even though she didn't usually harness horses herself, she had spent enough time in the stables to know the procedure. She was an even better driver than John, and she made her way through the still-muddy streets without problem.

As the morning clouds gave way to bright sunshine, Elizabeth tried to tell herself that John would be all right. But fear lay heavy on her as she drove along the same streets they had covered yesterday. She met sentries at two checkpoints, but with her passes and her smile, she managed to get past them, and she controlled her Virginia drawl as much as possible.

The next checkpoint was a different story. Somehow she had come too close to the White House.

"Ma'am, you're on federal property," the young corporal told her sternly, stepping up to grab hold of the horse's bridle. "You've no business here."

"Oh, dear." Elizabeth ached to lash out with her whip at his impertinent grip. She could feel the itch in her palm. Instead, she gave him her widest smile and batted her thick lashes. "I must have taken a wrong turn."

Another soldier came closer to stare suspiciously at her. This time her charm wasn't working, Elizabeth decided, her heart beating fast.

"Thank you so much. If you would give me room to turn my horse?"

Though she was a skilled horsewoman, Elizabeth's nervousness made the procedure an awkward business.

When the two soldiers finally had her buggy pointing back the way she had come, Elizabeth tried to think where she could look for her brother next. She nodded to the two obviously exasperated sentries and picked up her reins again when a stern voice called, "Just a minute there!"

Elizabeth felt a prickle of dismay run up her spine. She sat very straight, trying not to allow guilt to show on her face. But she felt a flush rise on her cheeks as an older man walked up. His uniform had three stripes on the blue sleeve, and he was frowning.

"The young lady's lost, sergeant," the first sentry explained.

"Is she now?" The sergeant looked at her, his eyes narrowed. "And where are you hailing from, miss?"

At another time, she would have smiled to hear his broad Irish accent. But just now, Elizabeth did not feel like laughing. Lucy's staid old horse, perhaps sensing her tension, tossed its head and pulled at the bit, whinnying shrilly.

"W-what do you mean?" She tightened her hold on the driving reins. Would they throw her in jail just for being in the wrong place? Would her Virginia birthplace brand her as a spy?

"Be your homeplace in Washington City, now?"

Hesitating, Elizabeth debated whether to lie. But she knew little of the city. He would find her out at once. She tried to sound confident.

"Are you saying that we may not ride through our own capital? Have things come to such a pass? It's a disgrace, I must say."

He did not appear impressed. "Putting aside the blarney, miss, I asked where you be hailing from?"

Elizabeth put up her chin, totally uncertain what to say next. But a familiar voice broke in.

"At ease, Sergeant. The lady is with me."

The sergeant whipped to attention, saluting the man who walked up behind them.

Elizabeth felt a shock of disbelief. The tall form, the broad shoulders, the dark eyes and hair—she had been searching for him ever since they had entered the capital, but now she couldn't trust her eyes.

Adam Cranfield tied his bay to the back of the buggy and swung a booted foot up. "I'll take the reins, my dear," he told Elizabeth, his tone polite, only his dark eyes glittering with amusement.

She had no choice but to hand over the leads and allow him to sit down beside her. Adam flicked the leather lines, and the horse moved obediently into a smooth trot.

Neither one spoke till the sentries had been left well behind. Then she turned to gaze at him. "Where did you come from? And why did you come to my rescue?"

He looked rueful. "I've been following you for blocks–I couldn't believe it was really you. And I thought perhaps I owed you that. We didn't have time for a thorough apology in Charleston. I did treat you shamefully on the beach that night."

"Did you? I barely remember."

"Indeed? I've had a hard time forgetting it. Do you receive so many moonlit kisses, Miss Stafford?"

He could make her angrier than any other man she'd ever known. Elizabeth jerked her shoulders back, once again wishing for her hand on the whip.

"Oh, very well, I *was* angry. I wanted to tear you into little shreds and feed you to the fishes. To use me like that for your own selfish purposes—" Then she remembered just why she had been combing Washington today, and she felt her face go even hotter.

His glance was ironic. He always seemed to understand too much.

"Not to worry—your troops wrought revenge enough on your behalf," Adam told her, his tone deceptively light. "They nearly roasted us alive at Sumter."

Elizabeth gave him a quick look. She saw the still-healing burn on his cheek and the grim lines around his mouth. Did his surrender still rankle?

"Why are you here?" he asked, his tone suddenly serious.

"I always take a morning drive." She turned her face away.

"To Washington City?"

"I'm visiting a cousin who is ill," she answered quickly.

"Then shouldn't you be home looking after this sick relation? This is not the best time to see the sights," Adam warned her. "I think I should take you home."

Meekly, she gave him directions to Lucy's house. With Adam in his blue uniform, the passage through the sentries was easy. As they approached Lucy's small brick residence, Elizabeth saw Adam look toward her once more.

"Mind you, if you had an escort, you could take a stroll now and then. How long do you stay?"

"I'm not sure," Elizabeth told him. "But my cousin is well enough to receive callers."

"Oh, is she?"

She thought she saw the slightest smile playing at the corners of his mouth. "When did you become so polite?" she demanded.

"A young lady told me I needed to mind my manners," he told her cheerfully.

Elizabeth flushed. He pulled up in front of the house. "Till tomorrow?" Adam said. "About three?"

Elizabeth struggled not to smile too broadly. "Charmed."

As he untied his horse and mounted swiftly, she saw the gleam of sunlight on his polished boots, the sparkle of the insignia on his shoulder. The air seemed to smell cleaner, even the drying streets appeared smoother. With an ironic salute, he rode away.

Then Elizabeth remembered John. How could she have forgotten his peril? But as she drove around to the stables, she saw their own carriage and her brother climbing slowly down, his limp more pronounced than usual.

"John! Where have you been? Are you all right?" She flung herself down from the buggy, letting the reins fall. The old horse simply waited patiently.

Her brother's face looked pale and drawn. She helped him out of his overcoat.

"I spent the night in jail," he told her, his voice hushed, with a glance toward the street. "I finally had a–a friend convince the authorities to release me this morning. Lucy warned me not to be on the streets, but I had–things to do. But in this city, with a war declared, my Southern birth makes me suspect."

"John, *whom* are you spying for?" Elizabeth blurted the question, then wished she had been more circumspect.

He looked at her closely.

"I won't tell on you, I promise," Elizabeth told him. "But I have to know."   "I support the cause I believe in, Elizabeth," John told her quietly, "and I don't wish you to know more. No need to endanger you."

Not John as well! Did no one give her credit for any sense? Did she always have to be protected, just because she was female?

"I had more I wished to do, but I fear we have to start for home tomorrow, Elizabeth."

Elizabeth swallowed a protest. No need to argue now. John looked exhausted. But after he was rested and fed, she'd convince him that he should return home without her.

"I'll be fine, really," she told him after breakfast. "I'd much rather visit with Lucy than quarrel with Father."

"With all the unrest, anything could happen," John protested. "How can I leave you?"

"You'll have a good excuse to come and fetch me in a month," Elizabeth told him. "And I'll just be a young lady on holiday, that's all."

John peered at her over his wire spectacles. He knew her too well, Elizabeth thought.

"Promise me, Elizabeth, that you will be sensible and do nothing rash."

"Of course," she told him, her tone earnest. She would have promised anything. She only knew that nothing and no one could have made her leave Washington now that she had found Adam again.

Early the next morning, John drove off in their carriage. Elizabeth had scribbled hasty letters to be mailed when he returned to Virginia, to Rosamund and Victorine, to Madame Corday with a note inside for Fanny to deliver to Hannah–and a cheerful but somewhat evasive note to Stephen.

The thought of Stephen evoked whispers of guilt inside her. His misconception about their betrothal nagged at her, but she hadn't the heart to tell him the truth about her feelings. She had convinced him to wait until the war ended to ask her father's permission for the marriage.

And when the war is over, Elizabeth promised herself, when he's no longer in danger, I will tell him. Then he can find himself another girl to devote himself to, someone to love him as he should be loved.

She spent the morning helping Lucy air the sheets and sort laundry. After a light luncheon, she watched the street through the parlor window, occasionally stopping at the looking glass in the hall to check her hair and give her cheeks a pinch to heighten their color.

Lucy watched her for a time without speaking, but at last she demanded, "This mysterious visitor you mentioned–it's a young man, isn't it?"

"What?" Elizabeth looked at her cousin in surprise.

"I'm not blind, my dear. You were so anxious to get your brother off–it must be someone your father does not approve of. Who is he?"

Elizabeth laughed. Lucy had fought her own battles with her family, after all. "He's a Yankee lieutenant, and his name is Adam Cranfield. I met him in Charleston at Madame Corday's Christmas ball. I saw him by chance yesterday when I went for a drive. That's when he said he would call."

Her cousin nodded slowly over her knitting of baby clothes. "If Madame Corday invited him to her house, I will trust his family and his character. Very well, I'll play chaperone for you, Elizabeth."

Elizabeth gave her cousin a quick hug, careful of the knitting needles. "You're a darling!"

Then she heard the sound of the brass knocker and walked–not too quickly–to open the front door herself.

His uniform was immaculate, his dark hair neatly brushed, his boots gleaming. He had brought a small bunch of daisies, probably picked from one of the open fields dotting the capital. Elizabeth thought she had never seen such a lovely offering.

"I'm so glad you could come," she murmured, giving him her hand.

His expression, which had looked almost guarded, lightened.

Lucy came forward to be introduced.

"I'm so glad to see that you're recovering," Adam told her politely, but his dark eyes had the usual sardonic gleam.

Lucy's quick laughter bubbled over. "I've a very resilient constitution," she assured him, "and Elizabeth's presence has worked wonders."

They chatted briefly, then Adam invited Elizabeth to stroll along the brick street. They took a turn along the avenue, walking in silence. Adam seemed short on words now that they were alone.

Elizabeth gazed at him.

Finally he met her glance, his smile hesitant. "I wasn't sure you wanted me to call."

"I wasn't sure you would come," she confessed. "But I hoped you would."

He seemed to relax a little, and she tucked her hand inside the crook of his arm. She could feel the hard muscle beneath the scratchy wool uniform. He put his other hand over hers. "At least you're on my territory," he told her. "You're on enemy ground this time, Miss Stafford."

His words brought back unpleasant memories of the fear she had felt during her search for her brother. Did their birthplaces make them foes? Why did it have to be like this?

She stopped and turned to face him. He stared down at her in obvious surprise. "It was only a jest," he said. "Don't look so alarmed."

"But it's not," she answered slowly. "Soldiers are standing guard right here in this city. I was almost arrested because of my Southern accent. I must tell you, I have come to believe that slavery is wrong—"

"Good for you," he interrupted. "For a plantation belle, you're growing very wise."

"But I'll always care for my homeland, despite its faults. I am still a Confederate at heart."

Adam grinned. "I wouldn't want you to be any less than you are," he told her. "I don't always understand you, Elizabeth. But you are unique—usually unexpected, never boring."

"So we are not enemies, Lieutenant Cranfield?"

His dark eyes met her own. "Not if I can help it," he promised, his tone serious. He reached for her hand again. She felt his grip tighten.

He stood very close. She could see his chest rising and falling rapidly, hear the faint exhalation of his breath. He smelled of wool and soap. Elizabeth found it hard to breathe.

He leaned closer, a question in his eyes. His touch on her hand was gentle, now, as if he wanted no hint of coercion. She could easily have stepped back. Instead, she lifted her face to meet his.

His lips were firm against her own. For an instant she savored his touch, then she returned his kiss with matching fervor. Adam pulled her even closer. A jolt that might have been as intense as a blaze of flame ran through her entire body, her knees felt weak, her belly hollow. Yet even as she startled at the new sensations, she also felt as if she had come home after a long and difficult journey—as if she belonged within his arms.

When he released her at last, Elizabeth felt weak. She could have sworn the sun was brighter, the birds' song more joyous.

"Not enemies, Elizabeth," Adam Cranfield told her softly. "Never again."

They walked slowly back to the town house, to tea and plum cake and polite conversation with Lucy. But occasionally, Elizabeth met Adam's gaze over the tea table, and the gleam in his dark eyes made her blush and smile. *Not enemies.*

## Chapter Ten

Adam came almost every day for the next two weeks. In the afternoon they walked or drove, all three squeezed into Lucy's one horse buggy. When military duties prevented an earlier visit, he came in the evening. The first night they looked at views of Niagara Falls in the stereoscope.

The next evening Elizabeth read aloud, and she and Adam argued amiably over their favorite authors.

"And Will Shakespeare, of course," Elizabeth said. "What's your favorite play? Mine is *Hamlet*, I think."

"*Romeo and Juliet*," Lucy put in.

"*The Taming of the Shrew*," Adam said, his dark eyes twinkling.

"Oh, you!" Elizabeth picked up a plump sofa cushion and tossed it at him.

He ducked hastily, and it fell harmlessly to the rug. "Auditioning for the part?"

Lucy's laugh rang out, and Elizabeth felt her cheeks burn.

"Here, you two," Lucy told them, opening a cupboard. "Try some parlor games and spare my pillows."

"Jackstraws! I'll take you all on." Elizabeth sat down at the small parlor table, and Adam and Lucy joined her. But it was Elizabeth's nimble fingers that won the match.

"We need a grown-up game," Adam declared, shaking his head over his defeat.

"We have Nathan's chess set," Lucy suggest. "If you know the rules. I confess I don't."

"Not I," Elizabeth said.

"I'll teach you," Adam offered. "And you, also, Lucy."

"Not me, I gave up on chess long ago. You two try your luck." Lucy went back to her sewing basket, and the lesson began.

But Elizabeth didn't have patience enough for the game. "Why can't I move my queen?" she demanded after a time. "She's the most powerful player, isn't she?"

"So they say." Adam's tone was dry.

Puzzled, she stared at him.

"I mean, if you move her so, my bishop will take her prisoner." He demonstrated on the inlaid wooden board.

Elizabeth shook her head. This talk of war and armies seemed too close to the real thing.

"I'd rather make my own rules," she announced.

Sewing sedately on the other side of the room, Lucy laughed. "That sounds like the Elizabeth I grew up with," she commented, reaching for her pincushion.

"You can't," Adam repeated, running his hand through his dark hair and leaving the careful waves disordered.

"Then I'll move my knight–so."

"And I'll take your knight with my pawn."

"No!" Elizabeth's impulsive movement jarred the board, and half the pieces went flying. Adam stooped to pick them up, disappearing beneath the table.

Flushing with vexation at her carelessness, Elizabeth also sank to the floor, though with some difficulty caused by her billowing skirts. The sight that met her eyes was worth her effort.

She found Adam stretched along the braided rug, marshaling his forces like a little boy lining up his toy soldiers. The sight of him so unguarded, so unlike his usual cautious self, filled her with a stab of affection.

"I'm so sorry. Is the knight injured?"

"Only in his feelings," Adam said softly. "The queen has been most unkind."

"She didn't mean to be." Elizabeth lowered her voice, as well. "She has the highest regard for the knight and would never treat him so shabbily. But the queen doesn't always think before she acts. She's a heedless wretch, I'm afraid."

"But a very special lady, nonetheless." Adam looked up and smiled at her, then reached across the rug and grasped her hand. His fingers were warm, his grip firm. She felt his strength and quiet determination as clearly as she ever had and glimpsed a tenderness he usually kept hidden.

"Good gracious, children, are you playing on the rug, now?" Lucy's merry call sent them both scrambling to their feet.

Elizabeth took her seat again, and, to cover her confusion, said, "You must have been a delightful little boy–your mother's darling."

Adam shrugged. "Hardly." His walls seemed to go up abrutly, and his easy playfulness disappeared.

Elizabeth bit her lip. She had said the wrong thing. She remembered his comment about Southern women and especially, his mother. Why did he have such painful memories?

But the ease between them had been destroyed. Not until he rose to go, and they walked a little way toward the door, did Elizabeth gather her courage again.

"What happened with your mother?" she asked him bluntly. This time she was prepared for the icy look.

"My mother was a gentlewoman from Virginia," he told her curtly. "The cold winds of New England did not agree with her health."

"You said as much before." Elizabeth refused to be put off. "But if she was in ill health, why do you hold it so against her?"

Lucy was putting away her sewing, preparing to bid their guest farewell. They had only a moment. Elizabeth thought he would not answer. When he did, his voice was quiet.

"My mother was a wounded butterfly, and she made everyone around her suffer for it. I grew up trying to easy her hurt, thinking it was somehow my fault, that if I did the right thing, it would make her sadness go away. But I never could. She died when I was twelve."

His look was too fierce to allow for pity. But she felt the pain and anger that still haunted him.

"That is why you distrust Southern women?" She met his gaze squarely. His dark brown eyes met hers, and what passed between them, she could not have explained. She held her breath.

Then Lucy joined them, and the spell was broken.

"Do come again," Lucy told Adam. "In fact, Elizabeth will celebrate her seventeenth birthday tomorrow. We're having a special dinner–I hope you can join us."

Her heart beating faster, Elizabeth waited for his answer. Had she offended him? Would their blossoming affection be blighted by the reminder of old pain? Most important, would he ever trust her completely?

But he returned Lucy's smile. "I should be honored."

The next day Elizabeth dressed with special care in her favorite green-trimmed white gown and brushed her chestnut hair until it shone.

But he did not come.

She waited for hours, and all the while terrible thoughts filled her mind. She'd brought up painful memories. Perhaps Adam had decided seeing her was a mistake. Why hadn't she minded her tongue, for once?

Nearly frantic, she paced up and down the parlor. Finally, she thought of another reason for his absence.

"Do you suppose the army is moving?" Elizabeth peered through the lace curtains at the parlor window.

"I don't know. The newspaper reports small engagements in the area, but nothing serious since the federal troops moved into western Virginia. Nathan heard from a friend in the government that General Scott expects to spend at least a year getting the new volunteer forces ready to fight. They're farm boys and shopkeepers, not soldiers, in no shape for battle. Surely the Confederate forces are as raw."

"I should think you're right," Elizabeth agreed, remembering Stephen's enthusiastic but ill-trained troops. "But things don't always go as planned. I wish I knew where Adam is."

"Come and eat some cake," Lucy begged. "And I made chicken croquettes, your favorites."

"It was very kind of you, but I couldn't swallow a bite—I have no appetite." Elizabeth stared at the sunlit street. "Oh, I hear something!"

Picking up her skirts, she ran for the front door and on to the brick street. Lucy followed more sedately.

At the end of the block, Elizabeth saw a cloud of dust and heard the tramp of marching men.

"They're moving troops!" she exclaimed. "I have to go see."

"Wait for me," Lucy called.

But Elizabeth couldn't restrain herself. She ran to the end of the street, her stays digging into her sides, stopping out of breath when she reached the broader thoroughfare.

The street was filled with Union soldiers, in many different uniforms, marching as merrily as if this were only another civic parade. Their ranks were uneven, and Elizabeth saw two men drop out to rest a moment in the shade of a tree, and another pause to accept a pitcher of water from a patriotic matron at the side of the road.

It was a warm day to be marching off to war, with the sun bright overhead. Elizabeth felt for the men in the blue or gray or red wool uniforms, many with high collars, loaded down with heavy haversacks and rifles. Where was Adam? Did he ride alongside his troop–off to battle? The thought chilled her.

They stood there for over an hour, till Lucy, flushed by the heat, suffered a wave of dizziness. Reminded of her duty, Elizabeth helped Lucy back home. After a glass of water and a cold compress to her head, Lucy soon recovered. Elizabeth's head ached the rest of the day, pounding like the slow rhythm of marching soldiers.

Before the sun set, Elizabeth heard a faint knock at the door. She hastened to open it and found a small boy staring up at her, his eyes big in his dirty face.

"Yes?" Elizabeth asked, puzzled.

"The lieutenant told me to come and tell you—" He hesitated.

Elizabeth urged him on. "Tell me what?"

"He had to go off and fight, maybe and he's awful sorry—"

"Not to come to dinner," Elizabeth finished for him, feeling her heart drop. "You took your time about it."

The urchin nodded cheerfully. "Maybe you got a coin for me?"

"I suspect you're been well paid, already," Elizabeth told him dryly. The boy nodded again. Relenting, Elizabeth told the child, "Come to the kitchen and I'll find you some bread and butter and a glass of milk."

Grinning, he nodded again. Elizabeth's steps were slow as she went to the kitchen to feed the waif and then, leaving him with the house maid, she went to tell Lucy of the message. Was Adam on the battlefield already?

The rest of the week crawled by with maddening slowness. Newspapers and gossip told rumors of limited engagements, while all of the capital seemed poised on the brink of crisis. Elizabeth nearly wore a path in poor Lucy's rug, pacing up and down, tortured by the forced inactivity.

On Saturday, July 20, she was aggrieved to see Lucy's next door neighbor riding off with his wife in a carriage loaded with hampers of food. "We're going to Centreville to view the army's movements," Mr. Waterson told them, his tone merry. "We'll bring you a report."

"Madness," Lucy muttered, sitting safely in her own armchair.

But when the Watersons returned unscathed that evening, with tales of faint cannon fire and troops maneuvering, Elizabeth felt even more exasperated. "Mrs. Waterson said the meadow was covered with people watching the show."

Lucy shook her head. "McDowell's Union army is camped at Centreville, at least twenty miles from here–too far from the city for me."

Sunday dawned bright and clear. Elizabeth could contain herself no longer. Rising early, she dressed in her riding habit. By the time Lucy came downstairs, exclaiming in surprise, Elizabeth had packed a large basket with cold meats and bread and fruit pie.

"Elizabeth, this is pure folly," Lucy scolded, standing in the doorway.

"I can't bear it," Elizabeth answered, her voice calm. "I hate being left out, and half the city is there. The Watersons have gone, and the Gilberts."

"Two neighbors do not make up half the city," Lucy argued. "I shudder what Nathan would say about this foolishness."

Lucy's elderly house maid nodded, but Elizabeth ignored them both.

"That's why you are staying here. With an early start, it will be only a pleasant drive. I'll spend a few hours and be home before dark." Elizabeth folded a clean tablecloth over the food. "I've made a crock of lemonade."

Lucy looked resigned. "Let me change my dress. I can't let you go alone."

Elizabeth hitched up the mild-mannered old horse and had the buggy loaded by the time Lucy came out, followed by her maid, who was wringing her hands.

"If you get yourself hurt, whatever will I tell Mr. Nathan?" Milly scolded.

"Don't worry, we'll be fine," Elizabeth predicted with easy confidence. She helped Lucy step up into the buggy, then climbed up herself. Flicking the leads, she urged the horse into its fastest pace, a slow trot. They soon joined the procession of carriages and wagons heading for the battlefield.

Swept along with the crowd of curiosity seekers, they drove slightly farther than Elizabeth had intended, a few miles past Centreville. Humdreds of Washington residents were settled with their hampers of food on the grass not far from a little stream called Bull Run. From this vantage point, they listened to the boom of the cannon and watched birds in a far line of oak trees rise squawking in alarm as rifle shots rang out.

Past the trees, the gray-blue line of the Blue Ridge Mountains could be seen clearly, despite the white puffs of smoke rising from unseen armament. Cannon roared like thunder, making Elizabeth's ears ring and reminding her unpleasantly of Sumter.

Yet the Washington thrill seekers laughed and talked as if they were theatregoers gathered to watch the latest play. Once in a while soldiers came into view as regiments waited for their orders or stragglers sat down to rest.

Elizabeth hobbled the horse, even though he was too placid to stray, gave him corn and water, and settled Lucy in the shade of a small tree with a plateful of food and some lemonade. Then she spent an hour wandering amng the crowd, trying to gather information about the battles.

As she listened to the lighthearted banter, Elizabeth felt a small chill inside her. She remembered the fierceness of the battle at Fort Sumter, and once again she feared for Adam's life. Now she knew that her attraction to him had been real. She would never feel this way about anyone else. She touched the brass button strung on a narrow ribbon around her neck and tucked it discreetly back inside her high-necked riding habit.

Before long she returned and sat down alongside her cousin. "The Union army is fighting the Confederates by Bull Run, a few miles from Manassas Junction. It's thought that Union forces plan to cut the rail lines at Manassas and move on to take Richmond, the Confederate capital.

"Some here think the Confederates are already on the run. Some say both armies are holding their ground. The people here–

I met two Congressmen in the crowd, just fancy–expected the army to be in Richmond by tomorrow. They think the federals will defeat the whole Southern rebellion in only one battle."

Lucy shuddered. "Look at the smoke cloud over the trees. Is that from cannon fire?"

"Probably. They say the Confederates are bringing in more troops by rail, although the Union forces are believed to still outnumber them."

Lucy looked pale, and Elizabeth had an attack of conscience. "I should not have allowed you to come, not in your condition."

"You should have stayed home yourself," Lucy answered, her tone tart. "I'm not worried about myself. But the thought of all these men shooting at each other. . . ."

They were both silent. Elizabeth sent up a silent prayer for Adam's safety and for the other soldiers, as well, whichever side they fought for. Sumter had been an almost bloodless battle. Did anyone really expect that good fortune to continue?

A sudden outbreak of shooting made her jump. This gunfire sounded much nearer than any battle sounds they had heard so far. She watched the road that led to Stone Bridge, only a few yards away. Soon Elizabeth saw bunches of men running toward them in disorganized fashion, followed by Union wagons and the ominous sight of ambulance wagons, all hurrying up the road.

"Are they retreating?" Lucy asked in alarm.

"We should start back," Elizabeth said. "Here, get into the buggy. I'll put the basket in."

Helping Lucy up, she tossed their supplies into the rear, unhobbled the horse, and climbed into the vehicle.

Around them, other spectators were also hastening to pack up and head for home. This war-side theater had suddenly grown too close to the action for comfort.

"Get up," Elizabeth called to their elderly steed, urging him into the procession of wagons and carriages that already crowded the road. More troops flooded out of the trees, covering the countryside, troops no longer as fresh and neatly clothed as the ones she had seen marching through Washington days before.

These men were smudged with smoke and reeked of gunpowder. The satin banners that had been marched out so proudly were now tattered and ripped by bullets. The men broke rank and began to run.

The sightseers did not help the situation. Ahead of Elizabeth, a man lashed his team until the horses jerked to the side, almost running the women's buggy off the road. Lucy squealed in alarm, and Elizabeth struggled to guide their horse back onto the track.

A sudden explosion shook the ground. Lucy screamed while Elizabeth clung grimly to her leads, steadying her horse.

"We're being shelled!" someone shouted.

A mounted civilian, his hat slipping off his head, was tossed off his horse as it reared in alarm.

"It's the Black Horse Cavalry—the Confederates are upon us. We'll all be shot!" someone called out in fear. "The shell hit a wagon on the bridge."

A wagon guided by a bearded, heavyset man tried to break into the line and crunched heavily against the side of their buggy. Lucy cried out in dismay.

"Mind your wagon!" Elizabeth shouted, pulling hard on her leads. She felt their entire buggy lurch as a wheel wobbled, then the whole buggy tipped. They were tossed into the milling traffic.

Elizabeth hit the road with an impact that took away her breath. Fighting for a moment to draw air into her lungs, she pushed herself to a sitting position. Her hair in her face, eyes gritty with dust, she cursed herself for the impulse that had brought them here. Where was Lucy?

A cry answered her thoughts. Elizabeth scrambled to her feet, barely in time to step in front of her fallen cousin and ward off a team of horses bearing down upon them.

"Hie!" she shouted, waving her arms at their heads. The horses reared and shied nervously aside.

She reached down to help Lucy up. Fortunately, her cousin had fallen toward the side of the road and hit a grassy bank.

"Are you hurt?" Elizabeth pulled Lucy away from the horses' hooves and grinding wheels all around them. *If Lucy loses her baby because of this, I'll never forgive myself!*

Lucy was pale, with a bloody scrape on the side of her face and tear stains showing through the dust on her cheeks, but she had regained her composure. "I'm all right. But how will we get home, Elizabeth? The bridge is blocked."

"You're going to get home," Elizabeth said, her tone grim. "Let me check the buggy."

The right wheel lay useless in the dirt, but Lucy's faithful old nag stood patiently in his traces and seemed unhurt, except for some scratches on his legs.

Elizabeth found a knife in the overturned food basket and sawed at the traces until he was free. Stepping over the shattered pieces of an apple pie, she guided the old horse into the field, where Lucy dabbed her handkerchief at the blood on her cheek.

"Drop your hoops," Elizabeth told her.

"What? In the middle of the field, for everyone to see?" Lucy sounded scandalized.

"You can't ride with them," Elizabeth explained patiently. "You can stand behind me. No one's looking. Hurry."

Lucy flushed, but she nodded. In a few moments, it was done.

"Up with you." Elizabeth laced her fingers together to brace her cousin's step, then lifted her up and across the horse's broad back.

"I've ridden him before," Lucy gained her balance and patted the animal's neck affectionately. "He's such a rock. But what about the river?"

"It's not that deep," Elizabeth told her. She held the reins and urged the horse forward around the congestion on the road, where men still shouted and argued.

She led the steed and its precious burden down to the small stream and scrambled up behind Lucy. The horse, now carrying them both, walked calmly into the water, swimming the few feet without any problem.

They clambered up the bank and headed back toward the road. On the other side of Cub Run, a Union soldier sat on a rock, his face blank, his blue eyes staring.

"What's wrong?" Elizabeth called, not sure why he looked so dazed.

Then she saw the blood dripping slowly from the wound in his chest.

"You must get help," she said, feeling her stomach lurch at the sight of the crimson blood staining his blue coat. The man was bleeding to death in front of her eyes.

The private did not answer. He didn't seem to hear.

Lucy was weeping quietly. "What can we do. Call one of the ambulances for help, Elizabeth."

Elizabeth looked at the turmoil behind them. "No one will hear," she said, her voice hollow. For a moment she hesitated, then she pushed herself off the broad back of the old horse, her feet hitting the ground with a slight thud.

"Elizabeth! What are you doing?"

"I'm going to try to help him. Madame taught us about binding wounds." Elizabeth's voice was as steady as she could make it. "You're coming home right away."

"I can't leave you in this, so close to a battlefield!" Lucy's blue eyes were wide with misery and indecision.

"It's my fault we're here. You must, Lucy, for the baby's sake. I shall make my own way back. Go, now." Elizabeth slapped the horse firmly on its rump, and the animal plodded forward.

Lucy sobbed once, then nodded. "God keep you."

Elizabeth hurried back to the man sitting so rigidly on the rock. She pulled up her riding skirt and ripped a length off her petticoat. "I think you should lie down," she told him.

He didn't move, but when she reached to open his jacket, he slid slowly down the rock till he lay on his back in the dirt. Elizabeth knelt to reach him. The blood flowed sluggishly but without stopping. When she saw the wound, Elizabeth gasped. But this was no time to give in to her churning stomach. Taking a deep breath to steady herself, Elizabeth folded the ripped piece of cloth and pressed it firmly against the jagged hole in his chest. Would he live? She didn't know. She took his own shirt—what was left of it—and used it to form a binding to hold the bandage in place. She looked at her handiwork anxiously. The bleeding seemed stopped.

"You must lie still," she told him, "until there is room for you on the wagons."

He closed his eyes, and Elizabeth felt fear ripple through her. Was he dead? Then she saw the slow rise and fall of his chest. She leaned against the trunk of a small oak tree, weak with relief.

She waited beside him until a supply wagon rumbled past—had the bridge at last been cleared? Then she ran to stop the wagon.

"You need a ride, miss? Hop on," the graying sergeant called.

"Not me, there's a man gravely wounded. Can you take him up, please?"

The driver hesitated, but Elizabeth held his gaze till he nodded reluctantly. With the help of another soldier, the wounded private was carried to the wagon and laid in it as gently as they could manage.

"You'd better climb in, too, miss," the sergeant repeated. "No place for a female out here."

"No, there's no room," Elizabeth said, regretful but firm. "Go on, I'll get a ride from another wagon."

But first she might as well walk back to the overturned buggy and see if anything remained of its spilled contents. Elizabeth's throat ached with dryness, and her stomach felt hollow and weak.

The sun had passed its zenith sometime past, but the air was still hot and dusty from the passage of so many men and animals.

She stopped at the stream to wash the blood off her hands, then managed to slip back across the bridge between groups of retreating soldiers and wagons and the parade of panicked spectators. She found their overturned buggy and its contents, slightly trodden on but other untouched. Most of their food had been trampled into the dirt, but Elizabeth found a piece of bread in the corner of the basket. By great good luck, the crock of lemonade was unbroken and had only leaked a little past its cork.

She stepped off the road to the shade of a tree and gulped down some lemonade and, after blowing off the dirt, chewed quickly on the bread.

She didn't stop long, but the brief respite helped. Feeling slightly refreshed, she stood up, ready to look for a seat in a wagon headed back to the city. She could hear the booming of cannon still, but saw little shelling directly around them. Her fear had faded, despite the wild flight of the Union soldiers, but she had a long and dusty walk ahead if she could not beg a ride.

A young soldier, so covered in dust that she could hardly see the color of his uniform, stood in front of her.

"Beg pardon, ma'am," he said meekly. "But could you spare a swig of that there water?"

"It's not—I mean, I guess so."

"Not for me, ma'am," the private said, though he eyed the jug thirstily. "But my friend is hurt real bad."

Elizabeth's heart sank. She followed the soldier to another clump of trees. In the sparse shade lay a lanky young man soaked with his own blood. He was breathing in harsh gasps and moaned quietly.

Elizabeth gazed at the shattered remnants of what had been his legs and fought to control her stomach.

"Water!" he gasped.

She dropped to her knees and poured lemonade into her palm, since he could not hold the jug. He sipped a few drops of liquid, then laid his head back.

Staring at his wounds–far beyond anything she could help–Elizabeth held back tears. The wounded man blinked at her as she sat outlined by the slanting rays of sunlight.

"Are you an angel, ma'am?" he whispered, so low she had to stoop to hear. "Am I in heaven?"

"No, soldier," Elizabeth's voice wavered, and she had to swallow hard. "I'm not an angel, just a girl. But you're seriously wounded–please lie still."

He struggled to reach inside his jacket, but his weakness defeated him. His hazel eyes looked to her for help. Elizabeth opened his coat carefully. He had a Bible in his pocket. Elizabeth drew it out. The cover was sticky with blood.

"What do you want me to do?"

He pushed open the cover, and she saw his name and home address written there.

"Write to my mother, please, ma'am," he whispered. "Tell her I love her and died like a soldier."

Elizabeth nodded. She could not speak. She held his hand while the ragged breaths slowed. When they ceased, she laid the limp hand back at his side. Putting the small book carefully inside the bodice of her riding habit, Elizabeth struggled to her feet.

The dead soldier's friend had disappeared, but–looking around her–she saw other wounded littering the grassy ground. Some were beyond any assistance, but she saw wounds she guessed she might actually be able to help.

Elizabeth sighed. Turning her face away from the city, she went to work. Later she could not remember how many men she had done her best to comfort and aid. Dozens, scores, hundreds, even–she couldn't be sure.

She did know that she ripped every shred of her petticoat into bandages and used even the ruffle at the bottom of her skirt until more would have left her practically naked. Then she used pieces from the soldiers' own shirts and jackets to bind up wounds. The luncheon knife she had stuck into her waistband she used to rip cloth and sometimes to hack slender branches into splints, holding bones in place so that these men had a chance to struggle to safety.

Every time Elizabeth saw a wounded Union officer, she fought back fear. Once she saw a lieutenant with dark hair face down in the dirt, and she had to stop herself from screaming Adam's name. But when she rushed forward, a close look at the man's back calmed her. This poor man was dead, but he was not Adam.

She knew Adam's shoulders, the way his dark hair curled just a little at the back of his neck. Sighing in relief, she brushed away a fly buzzing around her blood-stained clothes and moved on.

She worked until the sunlight faded. Fatigue crept over her, and her arms and legs felt almost too heavy to lift. Still the wounded straggled in, and still she worked. She saw a doctor on the battlefield once, and orderlies gathering up the wounded, but the bleeding, dying soldiers outnumbered their helpers by an impossible score.

She had bound up one more ugly seeping wound and urged a corporal on his way when she felt someone grab her roughly from behind.

She gasped, more in surprise than fear. When she turned, she saw the face she had dreaded to see on every dead man on the field.

"Adam!" She fell into his arms, and he swayed under her limp weight. They sat down together in the dirt. Adam Cranfield shook her, his expression angry—what she could see of it. His face was streaked with blood and dirt, and he reeked of gunpowder. But he seemed whole, except for a raw scratch down his shoulder and a bloody, swollen foot. Elizabeth laid her face against his dirty coat front, too relieved for words.

"What are you doing here? I've been searching–I heard another soldier speak of a woman giving aid to the wounded in the middle of our retreat. A red-haired, ragged angel with a Virginia drawl, he said. I thought of you—I couldn't help it. Elizabeth, are you mad?"

"A fine welcome," she murmured. He could rage all he wanted. He was alive.

"You must get back to the city. You're not safe here. Nightfall is upon us. Anything could happen."

She had never felt safer, leaning against his chest, his arms around her. She wanted to stay right here and never move again.

"Elizabeth, you have turned everything I thought I knew about women upside down, but you must listen to me!"

The crackle of gunfire rang out, and she saw sparks shoot through the trees. Who was shooting? She was too tired to be afraid.

"Elizabeth!"

The darkness took her.

She awoke, confused, to find herself lying on a cot with a tent looming close over her head. The rough wool blanket beneath her scratched her cheek. Terrible sounds came from outside. Where was she? What was happening?

She lay there until memory returned slowly. Had she dreamed this terrible day? No, the bloodstained Bible was still tucked inside her jacket. She felt a surge of fear. Where was Adam?

Still lightheaded from weariness, she pushed herself up and found a tin cup full of tepid water by her cot. She drank it eagerly, her throat felt as if it was lined with cotton.

Then she marshaled her courage and pushed open the flap of the tent. She saw a small campfire and men clustered around it, and more tents beyond. She stared at the soldiers in the flickering light of the fire. Were those Confederate uniforms? Yes, she heard the Southern drawl as they spoke quietly to each other. Had had she gotten here?

Someone screamed.

The men at the fire didn't even turn their heads. But Elizabeth was compelled despite herself. She made her way, a bit unsteadily, toward the sounds. She found more tents crowded with wounded men who lay shoulder to shoulder on bloody blankets, some on the bare muddy ground.

The screams came again, and the wounded men shifted restlessly.

"They're ataking of his leg off, poor sod," a private muttered.

Elizabeth shuddered. Then, like the rest, she tried to turn a deaf ear to the sounds of battlefield amputation. Instinctively, she looked for something to do, some way to help.

Finding a tin bucket of water and a dipper by the doorway, she made her way through the wounded, giving out sips of water, wiping fevered faces with a damp cloth.

The men gazed at her in astonishment, but she shrugged their queries aside.

But the sight of the man lying at the end of the row made her drop the almost empty bucket against the hard-packed dirt. Beneath the dried blood, his hair had once been blond, and those clear blue eyes she knew all too well.

"Stephen!"

## Chapter Eleven

She dropped to his side, shaking with horror. "Oh, Stephen, what are you doing here? I thought you were still in Charleston."

"Elizabeth?" He looked at her with pleasure and not a trace of surprise. "Sent you a letter. Couldn't sit there and miss all the fun. General Beauregard is here, you know, lots of Carolina folk."

The letter must be waiting at the plantation in Virginia, Elizabeth thought. She'd never thought Stephen might be in danger. It was too unfair.

"Are you hurt badly?" She retrieved the bucket and gave him a sip of the water, wishing it were more, wishing she had the power to ease his pain and heal all his wounds.

He choked a little over the liquid. She looked under the blanket that covered the lower half of his body and blinked in dismay.

Dear Lord, not Stephen! She thought of the confident, heedless young suitor who had climbed the wall at the Academy for her sake and had scratched his wrist on the broken bottle. And she had laughed. How could she had doubted his courage?

Worse, why hadn't she confessed his misunderstanding over their betrothal? She'd thought that there would be time—much more time.

He was drenched with blood, sour with the smell of it. It lay in sticky droplets on his face. Elizabeth tried to wipe his face gently and found his skin very hot to the touch.

He grasped her hand. "Good for you to come, such short notice," he babbled. "We'll be married soon, won't we, Elizabeth."

His blue eyes were as trusting as always. The lump in her throat made it almost impossible to speak.

"Soon," she whispered. "Lie still, Stephen."

But he shifted restlessly on the pallet, and she could almost see the wave of pain that came with the movement. He reached out to grasp both her hands.

"It's a great victory, you know," His voice was hoarse. "Not quite what I expected, the battle, but I did my best."

"I know you did," she agreed, feeling tears creep down her cheeks, not daring to lift her hand to wipe them aside. He clung to her hands as if they were a lifeline.

"They almost pushed us back once, but Jackson held firm—like a stone wall. Stonewall Jackson, eh? I told you we'd whip those Yankees."

"Yes, Stephen." Her back ached with fatigue, but it was a small thing in this tent of agony and death.

"I heard the bullets fly past my head. They sounded like firecrackers. But I didn't think I'd be hit. Is my mother here?"

"No, Stephen," Elizabeth whispered. "Shall I give her a message?"

"Tell her not to worry. She cried so when I left Charleston, my sisters, too. Tell them to take care. I'll make them proud."

"They're proud of you already, Stephen. We all are."

He babbled off and on about the battle for another hour and then fell silent. His eyes glazed, then he shuddered and lay still. His hands still clung to hers, and Elizabeth sat for a long time before she could make herself pull them away from his grip.

Then she closed his fixed blue eyes and covered his boyish face with the blanket. She stood up and almost fell, finding her legs numb from sitting so long. Wobbling, she made her way outside the tent. The officers found her there later, sitting alone, staring past the campfire into the darkness.

They led her back to her tent, and she tried to ask about Adam, about a Union lieutenant who might have been with her when she was found. But they shook their heads.

Lying limp on the cot once more, the air warm and humid in the little tent, Elizabeth remembered the shots she had heard just before she collapsed. Had Adam been shot, also? Did he now lie alone and dying on the battlefield?

Inside the canvas, she wept quietly for Stephen, for Adam, for all the men who suffered and died in the darkness. Some time before dawn, despite the groans and screams of men from the hospital tents, she dropped into an exhausted sleep.

An army doctor, his eyes red rimmed with weariness, his uniform splattered with blood, came to see her the next day. There was little he could do except pat her shoulder, shaking his head over her swollen eyes and pale cheeks.

"We'll get you home, poor lass. This is no place for a lady. Though yesterday some of the men were thanking heaven you were there."

She should have felt some comfort at his words, but Elizabeth was too numb, sunk too deeply in anguish and loss. At her request, a message was sent to Lucy that she would not be returning to Washington City. She asked to have her belongings sent back to the plantation. It was time for her to go home.

Elizabeth hardly remembered the train trip back to Richmond. Her brother met her at the station with Uncle Elijah. He looked shocked when he saw her.

Their father stormed out of his study when they reached the plantation.

"Elizabeth Margaret, I've had a jumbled note from Lucy, but I don't understand any of this. How in blue blazes did you end up in the middle of a battlefield? What kind of behavior is this for a young lady?"

"I saved a man's life, I think," she told him calmly. "More than one, maybe, but many of them died, anyway. I'm too tired to argue."

Walking away from his expression of bewilderment and outrage, she slowly climbed the stairs to her own room. She put the soldier's Bible on her bureau. Clutching Adam's brass button, she sank into bed.

She slept for much of the next week, and even when awake, found it hard to think or plan. A letter from Lucy relieved her of worry about her cousin's health, but even that seemed distant now.

Her father blustered at her once or twice. She simply stood quietly and let the words rush past her. After what she had seen on the battlefield, her father would never look quite so frightening again.

Her unusual demeanor left William Stafford looking both exasperated and puzzled. Finally in September he sent her back to Charleston and Madame Corday's school.

John drove her to the station. "Are you going to be all right?" he asked with genuine concern. "You were very brave, little sister."

She nodded, reaching impulsively to hug him. He patted her shoulder. But as the train chugged away from Richmond, the weight of her loneliness and guilt returned.

When she reached Charleston, Madame was waiting at the station, with Rosamund and Victorine close behind. "Elizabeth, dear child." Madame Corday held out her arms, her expression full of love and compassion.

At the embrace, Elizabeth almost broke down. She closed her eyes for an instant, and the weight of unshed tears felt heavy against her lids. But something held her back.

"Elizabeth," Rosamund asked. "Are you all right?"

Afraid to trust to trust her voice, Elizabeth nodded.

"It is hard, yes, to lose one you love," Victorine said, her voice low.

Victorine almost understood. The lump in Elizabeth's throat grew even larger and more painful. She accepted their hugs, but she still couldn't tell them the whole story.

They drove her back to the Academy, gave her hot tea and a shawl for her shoulders. She felt as cosseted as an elderly lady. In truth, she felt old inside.

Later, she roused herself to visit Hannah, who was waiting eagerly at the shop.

"Miss Elizabeth!" But after the first greeting, Hannah's smile faded. "Lizbet, what's wrong?"

"I'm all right," Elizabeth murmured. "Just tired, still."

Hannah took her hand. Elizabeth felt the warmth and strength of Hannah's grip.

"I've seen that look before, most often in the slave cabins. Someone's bruised your soul."

The words trembled on the tip of her tongue, but Elizabeth couldn't get them out. Not even to Hannah could she put into words all the anguish that weighed her down.

Next, she visited Stephen's family, repeated his messages of love, and wept with his mother and three sisters. Back in Virginia she had written to the dead private's mother and mailed home his bloodstained Bible.

Now she tried to put the battle behind her. But the dreams wouldn't stop, dreams of Stephen smiling on his deathbed, dreams in which she tried to find Adam. Just as she caught a shadowy glimpse, he would disappear again into the mist. She woke often with wet cheeks and an intense sadness inside her.

Another letter came from Lucy. She was well, her husband was home at last, but there was no word from 'your chess tutor.'

So Elizabeth went back to life as it had been. Charleston was little changed, though there were fewer students at the Academy this year. Confederate forces held Fort Sumter and the other forts. The Union blockade had little effect as yet, except for high prices in the shops.

In early November, Port Royal, south of Charleston, fell to Union forces. Rumors of impending disaster swept the city, but the enemy troops didn't come. Elizabeth paid little attention. She sat dutifully through her classes, but her mind wandered, and she couldn't concentrate on her studies.

Madame looked concerned but didn't scold her. Finally, Madame Corday called her to her private study and nodded toward a chair. The headmistress, in a dove gray gown, smelled faintly of rosewater.

"Elizabeth, my child," she said. "I loved my husband dearly, and I lost him too young. I know you've been through a dreadful ordeal. I've left you alone, thinking you needed time for yourself. But you're still drifting, I think, in need of a helping hand. Would you like to talk? It might help."

Elizabeth perched on the edge of her chair and looked at Madame Corday's calm gray eyes, heard the serenity in her voice. How had she ever found peace again?

"You miss the young man who died? You're angry because you lost someone who might one day have become your husband?" Madame probed gently.

"Oh, no, I mean, it's so complicated," Elizabeth said quickly. At last, the whole story of the almost-betrothal came tumbling out. Madame listened gravely.

"I feel so–so guilty," Elizabeth told her headmistress, stumbling over the words she had been too ashamed to speak. "Stephen loved me, and he thought we were betrothed. I wronged him terribly, and now he's dead, and I can't change anything."

"What did you do that was so unforgivable, Elizabeth?" Madame's voice was kind.

"I let him think that I loved him. And I didn't love him, not really, though I tried."

"Did you deceive him out of malice?"

"Of course not. I didn't want to wound him." Elizabeth felt in her throat the familiar ache of unshed tears.

"Loving you made Mr. Hall happy. I can't see how you harmed him, Elizabeth. Love cannot be forced, only freely given. Stephen is at peace now. You must allow yourself the same blessing."

Elizabeth felt salty tears sting her eyes. She sobbed once, then added, "But there's Adam–Lieutenant Cranfield." She told Madame of the time they had spent together at her cousin's house, and his disappearance on the battlefield.

"Not knowing is so hard. I believe he would have written to me, if he could, at least let me know that he lived. But I've heard nothing. . . ." The tears came harder and even more bitterly than before.

Madame leaned over and put her arms around Elizabeth's shoulders, allowing her to weep until she felt empty and spent.

December came with little change in the war. The other girls talked of Christmas, but Elizabeth had no heart for a holiday. After her talk with Madame Corday, Elizabeth had confessed the whole story to Rosamund and Victorine and later to Hannah. They had wept with her and offered consoling words. Some of the weight within her had eased, but the worry over Adam's fate remained.

On the evening of December 11, Madame was called away by an urgent message from her sister. "My nephew is ill. I'm going to see if I can help. Fanny is here. She can fetch me if I'm needed, girls."

Elizabeth nodded and Rosamund helped Madame put packets of chamomile tea and quinine powder into a sweet-grass basket.

The big house felt strange with Madame gone. The girls went up to bed early, and Elizabeth had unbuttoned her waistband and bent to step out of her skirt when she heard the alarm bells ring. She hurried to the window and pushed up the sash, leaning out into the cool air.

"Fire!" Rosamund stood behind her, her voice tense.

Straining her eyes, Elizabeth could see the steeple of St. Michael's and the red signal light that shone there. "It's blocks away. Surely the fire companies will take care of it."

Rosamund wrinkled her nose. "I hope so. But most of the regular firemen have gone into the army, Elizabeth. And I've

heard the new steam-powered fire engine isn't even used. The fire
companies find it too new-fangled for their liking."

Elizabeth decided not to undress just yet. She pulled her skirt
back on. They sat quietly in their room and tried to read. But in a
little while Elizabeth heard the rattle of tree branches outside the
window.

"The wind's picking up," she told Rosamund, feeling a tremor
of unease. She went back to the window. She could hear
shouting. A dim red glow lit up the dark sky.

"I'm going to see how close it is," she told her friend, slipping
into a thick wool pelisse.

"Madame won't allow it."

"Madame's not here," Elizabeth reminded her.

Rosamund looked apprehensive. "Should we send Fanny to
tell her?"

"Surely she's heard the sirens. She'll likely be back soon unless
her nephew is too ill to leave. He's had the fever before.
Rosamund, get the younger girls up–make sure they're dressed
and ready to leave in case the fire gets this far."

Rosamund's eyes widened, but Elizabeth felt curiously calm.
She went downstairs, spoke to Fanny about gathering up some of
Madame's valuables, then went out the front gate and into the
cobblestone street.

She heard men shouting and the clamor of the fire. It seemed
closer. The wind was sweeping toward the school–a very bad
sign. Hurrying along dark streets lit only faintly by street lamps,
she could smell the suffocating smoke, hear the crackle and snap
of the blaze. When she saw it, she bit back an exclamation.

The fire had grown to monestrous proportions. The heat
could be felt from blocks away, and flames roared and whipped in
the wind, reaching out for more wooden buildings to engulf.

She saw men, black and white, working desperately on the
hand-pumped fire engines, but this fire would not be easily
quenched. With most of the regular firemen away in the army,

the war had managed to deal them a crushing blow, even though the nearest Union army was far away.

"It started at the sash-and-blind factory, perhaps by a refugee's campfire. Secession Hall's already gone," a man shouted as he pushed a cart full of valuables away from his home. "Once the roof catches, the building is lost."

Elizabeth saw a handsome sideboard, a Grandfather clock, and boxes and barrels of household goods, all balanced precariously on the small wagon. Beside the man, a woman sobbed as she helped wheel away what was left of the home. A small boy clung to his mother's skirts.

Elizabeth ran closer to the fire. The gyrating spirals of gold and crimson were terrible, but beautiful, too. The sight was almost hypnotic. She watched the flames dance and climb toward the sky until a flying spark stung her face, pulling Elizabeth from her trance. She could feel the heat against her face. The smoky air made her cough.

She started back. At Mills Hotel, she saw the manager and servants battling the blaze with buckets of water and determined faces. Wet blankets hung out many of the windows, flapping against the pink facade. A crowd of guests hurriedly evacuated the building.

She saw a face familiar from a newspaper sketch–the stately uniformed man with the graying hair and moustache was a Confederate general: General Robert E. Lee. He held a baby in his arms. As she watched, he returned the wailing infant to its mother, who babbled her thanks.

Elizabeth ran back toward the school. The fire was still spreading, and in a southwesterly direction. They must be prepared, or Madame Corday's home and all her possessions could be destroyed in minutes.

Back at the Academy, she found a knot of younger girls huddled in the front hall, whimpering and clinging together.

Behind them, Rosamund looked calm. Victorine was pale, but her expression was resolute.

"Fill all our buckets and bowls with water," Elizabeth said.

"We did that," Rosamund assured her.

"Then wet some blankets, and let's take the pails to the attic where we can get to the roof. Sparks are flying all over the block. If the roof catches, the whole house will go."

Leaving Fanny with the younger students, the three girls hurried up to the attic, burdened with sloshing pails of water. Elizabeth climbed through the same window they had used to watch the battle of Fort Sumter–how long ago that seemed!

Sparks were flying everywhere, drifting through the air like treacherous fireflies. Already several wooden shingles smouldered. Elizabeth rushed forward with her pail, drenching the wood. The other girls followed her example.

When their buckets were empty, they flailed at the sparks with wet blankets. Elizabeth's arms soon ached with the weight of the damp fabric, but so far, the roof remained whole.

"We have more water," someone called from the window.

Turning to look, Elizabeth saw Sarah at the window, a pail ready to hand out.

"We've made a bucket chain up the stairwell," the younger girl explained earnestly.

"Good for you, Sarah," Elizabeth told her. "Madame will be proud."

They worked for some time until a light rain began to fall over the city.

"We're saved!" Victorine said with relief.   They all climbed back inside the attic to rest. But the rain stopped too soon, and the fire was not yet out. They took their posts on the rooftop again.

Home at last, Madame Corday came to the attic window, her expression agitated. "Girls! Are you all right? My nephew's fever has finally broken. I thought we were going to lose him, this time. But this is too dangerous. We must send you away from the fire."

"No, Madame," Elizabeth begged. "We've held it off this long. We can't give in now."

Madame pressed her lips together. "Very well, but if the fire looks to surround us, you must go when I bid you."

It was a long and difficult night. When the sun rose, the devastation that met their eyes was so large that even Madame looked stunned. More than five hundred acres of the city had burned. Later, when it was counted, they learned that five hundred homes had been destroyed, as well as five churches, and many shops and businesses.

Madame Corday's Academy still stood, though the empty stable and another outbuilding had burned. But no one at the school was hurt, and Elizabeth felt a strange exultation. They had worked together and won against a foe even more deadly than the Union forces. If they could endure against this, surely life was not yet hopeless.

Elizabeth wiped her sooty hands across her cheeks, feeling the sting where sparks had touched her skin. She looked up when Rosamund laughed.

"If you could see your face."

Elizabeth stared at the black cinders and smoke that coated her friends from head to foot. They all stank of smoke and were damp with sweat and water. Victorine sniffed her own grimy hand and shuddered.

"I don't have to, I can see yours," Elizabeth answered. She and Rosamund laughed, and in a moment, even Victorine joined in.

Elizabeth ran down to the modiste's shop to make sure Hannah was all right, finding her working hard to scrub away smoke stains from the mostly intact building. Then she returned in time for her turn at the hip bath, and then some much needed sleep.

Then they helped Madame set up a soup line for the many left homeless from the fire. Elizabeth was stirring a hearty vegetable soup when Fanny called her to the door of the kitchen. Outside, she found Hannah waiting. They had not been able to talk, earlier.

"Hannah! I was so glad you are all right."

"And you? Fanny told me how hard you fought." Hannah touched a singed piece of hair that hung beside Elizabeth's cheek.

Elizabeth shrugged. "I did what I could."

"It was bravely done. I'm glad to see you with light back in your eyes. You're healing, at last. More than that, I think you've changed since the battle in Virginia."

Elizabeth raised her brows. "Why do you say so?"

"You were always impulsive and unafraid, ready to run into harm's way. But now you're stronger and wiser, and you think of other people more. Your heart has *growed*, Mama would have said. She'd be proud to see her little Lizbet growing into such a fine lady."

Elizabeth's vision blurred with tears. "Thank you," she whispered, swallowing the lump in her throat. "She'd be proud of you, as well, Hannah. I suspect no one could be braver or more resourceful."

It was Hannah's turn to blink hard. "I hope so. Someday I hope I can tell you everything, Elizabeth." They clasped hands for a minute, then Hannah said, "I must get back."

"Take care, Hannah."

Smiling, the other girl nodded, and Elizabeth went back to her soup.

They fed a long line of men, women, and children. But to Elizabeth's annoyance, Madame made them all stop work in the kitchen when the doctor came by at last.

It was not their usual doctor, who had joined the Southern forces and was now away with the troops. This man wore a Confederate uniform and looked vaguely familiar.

"Aren't you the young lady who worked on the wounded at the battlefield at Manassas?" he asked quietly as he examined the scrapes and minor burns on her arms and face.

Elizabeth flushed, but she nodded.

"I thought so. I'm glad to see you in good form, my girl. That Yankee who brought you in hasn't been as lucky, I'm afraid."

Elizabeth felt her heart lurch, then pound like an angry beast. She could hardly speak. "You know what happened to Adam—to Lieutenant Cranfield?"

The doctor's eyes were grave but kind. "He turned himself in to the sentries to get you aid. Did you not know? But the camp was in confusion that night. The officer in charge may not have connected the two events."

"Where is he? He isn't—"

"Dead?"

The pause was too long. Elizabeth thought her heart would burst.

"No, he had a foot wound, but it hasn't healed properly. He's doing poorly, I'm afraid. He's here at Castle Pinckney, with other Union prisoners from Manassas."

Adam, ill and a prisoner, and all because of her.

"Please, how can I see him?"

The doctor looked doubtful as he put away his salves and ointments. "A prison's no place for a lady."

"Oh, but I must visit him. He saved my life. I might be able to help him."

He gazed at her again. "Too bad you're not older, lass, and a good deal less comely. You'd make a fine nurse. Very well, I will write you a pass."

Elizabeth waited impatiently for him to hand over the precious piece of paper, then she ran to find Madame Corday.

"I must go right away, Madame," Elizabeth's words tumbled out. "I don't know how ill he is."

Rosamund and Victorine were listening as well. Rosamund looked sympathetic, but Victorine shook her head.

"To visit a Yankee prisoner? I know you cared for him, Elizabeth, but he is the enemy now. Besides, no one in town will speak to you. Those Northerners have been killing our men. Don't you care?"

"This Yankee is different, Victorine. And I don't care what the town thinks. Please, Madame!"

"You can't go alone, Elizabeth," Madame Corday answered. "And I simply cannot leave just now. I have hungry children, homeless from the fire, still to feed."

"I will go with her," Rosamund volunteered, her voice quiet.

The headmistress hesitated, and Elizabeth almost couldn't breathe. Surely Madame must see how important this was.

"Very well, but you must be home before dusk."

"Thank you!"

Elizabeth hugged Rosamund in gratitude, then hurried to find a basket. Victorine shook her head in disapproval, but she helped them pack bread and cheese and dried fruit and a small tin bucket of soup in case he was too ill to eat solid food. Madame stopped her own work long enough to measure out quinine and brew herb tea.

"This might help," she told them. "Do be careful."

As they walked to the harbor, Elizabeth saw that the town was so devastated, brick chimneys standing eerily alone amid the rubble, that at any other time it would have made her shudder. Now, although she pitied the victims of the fire, she had her thoughts centered on another person in peril.

It took them some time to find a boatman who would take them across the water to the island on which Castle Pinckney was situated. But finally they sat stiffly in a small boat braving the choppy winter waves.

Castle Pinckney was relatively small, a rounded fortress of brick and mortar. The Union guard seemed suspicious of their hand-written pass, but Elizabeth would have argued with the Devil himself. Nothing could keep her from Adam.

"Now, really, what do you think two mere girls can do—take over the castle with their bare hands? I have food for a sick prisoner."

"What's your interest in this man?"

"He's a distant relative," Elizabeth said firmly. The corporal looked very young and a little self-important with his military duties. "Now please take us to him."

They were handed over to another more cheerful soldier and taken inside the fort. Rough partitions of thin wood had been thrown up around the inner walls, with tarpaulins over the patchy roof. The shelters were drafty and cold.

Elizabeth shivered to think of Adam held in such bleak conditions. No wonder he was ill.

The smell of unwashed men and the sour stench of sickness met the girls as they came nearer. Elizabeth saw groups of men with tattered uniforms sitting besides the rough sheds.

"This is the one, I think. Yank, a lady to see you. Mind your manners."

They were allowed inside. Clutching her basket tightly, Elizabeth stepped into the dimness. A big, rough-looking man sat on the brick floor. He stared up at her in surprise.

"Blessed Mary, what's this, then?" he asked in a strong Irish brogue.

Elizabeth was already looking past him. In the back of the small room, a man lay on a narrow pallet, only one blanket covering his shivering body.

"Adam?"

He was so thin, his face pale and shaded with dark stubble. His uniform, always so neat and trim, had stains across its front and two buttons were missing. He smelled of sweat and illness, and his breathing rasped in his throat.

Elizabeth thought he was a beautiful sight, although at the same time, his obvious illness hurt her heart. She put down her basket carefully and knelt on the cold floor. "Adam, do you know me?"

She let her fingertips lightly rest on his forehead. His skin was hot and dry. Wetting a cloth from the jug of clean water they had brought, she wiped his face. His eyes opened. Adam stared at her.

"I'm dreaming again," he muttered hoarsely.

Had he been haunted by dreams, too? Elizabeth had to struggle to steady her voice. She gripped his hand, hoping her touch would convince him that she was real.

"No, it's Elizabeth. I've found you at last. Adam, I'm so sorry. It's all my fault that you are here. I should have stayed away from the battle. Can you ever forgive me?

He blinked, and she saw a spark of the old energy in his eyes.

"I met men that day who thought you were an angel. They were happy to see you at Bull Run. I've nothing to forgive. War has many surprises, mostly unpleasant. But your presence here makes up for many."

He gripped her hand, but his old strength was lacking, and just speaking left him breathless.

Elizabeth frowned in concern. "We've brought you food. Try to drink some soup."

As Rosamund helped her with the soup, Elizabeth spoke softly to the other prisoner, who was eyeing the basket with hungry eyes. "What's wrong with him, do you know?"

The big Irishman shrugged. "A fragment of cannonball hit him in the foot. Broke a bone, maybe, and t'wasn't set well. Now he's down with dysentery, camp fever. The usual."

"You're well?" Rosamund asked, offering him bread and cheese.

He accepted eagerly. "Ah, us Irish, we're tough lots, miss, especially the Sixty-nine Irish Regiment, that's my troop. But these New York boys—" He broke off to eat.

Meanwhile, Elizabeth spooned soup for Adam. Leaning on one elbow, he ate most of the soup they had brought, and she thought the nourishment brought some color back to his face. She gave him a dose of the bitter quinine powder, and he washed it down with weak tea, also from their basket. When he lay back down on the pallet, she came to a swift decision.

"As soon as you're well enough, we're going to get you out of here," she said, her tone firm.

"How?" Rosamund asked in surprise.

"I don't know, but I'll find a way. But this is no place for a sick man."

Even the thought of Adam leaving her to go back north made her hurt inside. Elizabeth pushed the pain away. His health and well being mattered more.

"I'll be back," she promised Adam.

He reached for her hand and held it, as if reluctant to allow her to leave. "Will you disappear into a dream again?" he asked in a low voice.

"Never," she answered, kneeling beside him and lifting his hand to her cheek. "Now that I've found you, I'll never let you vanish again."

He smiled and closed his eyes.

The trip back across the water was cold and windy. Elizabeth spent it thinking hard. As the chilly salt spray blew into her face and dampened her hair, and the gulls shrieked overhead, she plotted with all her old energy to find a way to free Adam.

## Chapter Twelve

"I know the general is busy," Elizabeth told the young officer. "But I've been sitting in this waiting room for days. This is important! A man could die while I'm waiting my turn."

"The fire—" the man began.

"I know about the fire. But my business won't take long. If I could just see the general for five minutes?" She gave him her most beguiling smile, but the young man shook his head.

Her temper barely in check, Elizabeth stalked back to her chair. For almost a week, trading on the doctor's pass, Elizabeth had spent every morning tending to Adam, taking him nourishing soup and seeing his fever ebb and some of his strength return. And every afternoon she had harassed a series of reluctant Confederate officers.

Madame Corday had not been happy about Elizabeth's obsession, but this time, the older woman had lost the battle of wills.

"I'm sorry, Madame, but it's something I must do," Elizabeth told her headmistress with calm certainty. Just as Hannah had discerned, Elizabeth had found her own inner strength at the Battle of Manassas, as most Southerners referred to it– Northerners called it the Battle of Bull Run. She would never again feel so childlike and helpless.

Madame Corday sighed and let her go. "War does turn our lives upside down," she said.

Rosamund had stood by her resolutely, traveling to the prison every morning to chaperon and aid, and spending her afternoons catching up on schoolwork. Hannah begged leave from the shop to come with her twice as Elizabeth visited Confederate offices. When the dressmaker objected and Hannah had to return to work, Elizabeth went alone.

As Elizabeth sat in the waiting room, she thought about how Victorine had remained disapproving, until a letter had arrived from home that had sent her into such an ecstasy of joy that she forgot about everything else. Elizabeth and Rosamund had returned from their third visit to the prison at Castle Pinckney to find Victorine waltzing around her bedroom, humming and clutching a letter to her heart.

"What on earth?" Rosamund demanded.

The sight was so strange that even Elizabeth had been briefly shaken from her own preoccupation.

"Voila–a letter from my papa!"

She shook the heavy sheet of paper.

"After Sumter's fall, and then the great fire, he doesn't feel Charleston is safe any longer. And New Orleans is still firmly in Confederate control, and the risk of fever is slight in the winter. I shall go home!"

"Oh, Victorine, we will miss you," Elizabeth said, genuinely sad at the thought of her friend leaving the school.

Rosamund nodded.

"And *moi aussi*, I will miss you both. But to go home–I have been so homesick. And there's more!" Victorine's brown eyes sparkled, and an unexpected smile lit up her heart-shaped face.

"Tell us," Rosamund urged, laughing a little at Victorine's contagious delight.

"Papa says he has found a young man, an exemplary young man, handsome and well bred, who is going to ask for my hand in marriage!"

Rosamund's smile faded, and Elizabeth was stunned. "Do you know this young man?"

Victorine's brow wrinkled. "I think I met him years ago–it's hard to remember."

"But, Victorine! You're going to marry a man you don't even know?" Rosamund sounded scandalized. "How can you do that?"

Victorine stamped her small foot. "But my papa has arranged it. Do you think he would select for me anyone but the finest husband?"

It was too European and medieval for Elizabeth's liking. She shared a worried glance with Rosamund. Despite all his apparent virtues, what if Victorine discovered she didn't even like this 'exemplary' man? But in the face of Victorine's acceptance of this arranged marriage, what could they say?

"I hope you're very happy," Elizabeth had told her friend, weakly.

At least it gave Victorine something else to think about, and she forgot to scold Elizabeth about 'consorting with the enemy.'

Elizabeth's thoughts jumped abruptly back to the present when the inner door to the office opened. A man came out whose erect posture and graying mustache were familiar to her.

"General Lee!"

He paused to smile courteously at her. "Yes?"

"I need a word with you, please, General."

To Elizabeth's relief and the orderly's obvious annoyance, the general waved her inside his office. General Robert E. Lee was not well known outside of Virginia, but Madame Corday had told Elizabeth that his character and military expertise were highly praised by professional soldiers. Gazing at him with respect, Elizabeth hurried to present her case.

"It's a Union officer in Castle Pinckney prison, sir. He was wounded, and he's been ill for some time. He should be released. Surely we don't have to fight sick men?"

She looked at him anxiously. The general sighed, and she hurried to explain about the battle in more detail, how Adam had surrendered to keep her from harm. As she told the story, General Lee regarded her closely.

"You're the young lady who treated the wounded at Manassas? I've heard that story."

Afraid to trust her voice, Elizabeth nodded. She had made the most fervent plea she could. She was tired and discouraged, and if this man turned her down, she feared Adam would die in his miserable prison cell.

"It's my fault, you see," she told the general, her voice husky. "It's only fair that Adam go home so he can recover."

"We've had some problems with prison exchanges," Lee told her. "The federal government seems to think that by exchanging prisoners in the normal way, they'll be recognizing the legitimacy of the Confederate government. They're determined not to do that."

Elizabeth felt anger overcome her despair. "Men have to die because of political wrangling?"

"I'm afraid that included much of the cause of the war, my dear," he told her gently. "But we have, in fact, released wounded prisoners from Richmond before this. I don't see why one more man cannot be sent home."

Elizabeth jumped to her feet, joy erasing all the fatigue and frustration of the week just past. "Oh, thank you, sir!"

He shook her hand. "I'll get the paperwork started. Herbert," he called to the young man outside. "Bring your pen."

Blinking her eyes against sudden dampness, Elizabeth squeezed her hands together in silent jubilation.

Getting Adam to agree turned out to be the next obstacle.

"Running home with my tail between my legs like a wounded dog," he fumed, although too weak to raise his voice. "A fine soldier I would be to do that."

Elizabeth frowned at him. "Do you think you're serving your cause by lying there and dying? You must, Adam! Don't be so stubborn."

She knelt beside his pallet, aware of his cellmate who watched them with open interest, and of Rosamund's more tactful presence. But she didn't care.

"I just want you to get well." She touched his cheek, scratchy with the uneven stubble of his beard. "Please."

She met his glance firmly, and for a moment they gazed at each other. Then—

She handed him the pen, and sighing, he scrawled his signature on the paper. She blew gently on it until the ink dried and wouldn't smudge, then she folded it carefully to give to the waiting sergeant.

Adam clasped her hand again. "I told you in Washington we were not enemies." His voice was low. "But I didn't realize even then the hold you would have on my heart."

Unable to answer, Elizabeth gripped his hand, almost forgetting the cold stone floor beneath them, the sour prison smell all around. She was aware only of his touch and the sound of his voice, low but resolute.

"I thought I knew women, especially Southern women. I thought they were frail and helpless, impossible to please. You have strength to spare and courage enough for an army. Your beauty and grace would shame a princess, yet you seldom seem to think of yourself. You've taught me I don't know women at all. You're inside my soul, Elizabeth."

She fought to hold back tears. "I have never loved a man as I love you. I know I never will again."

"So how can I leave you? I haven't the authority to take you with me now, even if I had the strength. Your father would never grant permission, and you're not of age to marry without it. If I go North now, with the war between us, I might never see you again!"

"I would go with you if I could, Adam," she told him. His grip tightened–her fingers were almost numb. But despite the painful pressure, she savored his touch, knew she would ache for it often in the long, lonely days ahead. Her own voice was hoarse with barely contained sorrow. "Because you love me, you'll do this."

"Leave you?"

She nodded, and in her memory heard cannon fire and the rapid popping of rifles, smelled gunpowder and the sharp odors of blood and death. In their anger and arrogance, they—North and South—had let war loose on the land. Now no one knew how many deaths it would demand, how many lives it would change forever.

But she could do something right this time, heal instead of hurt. That was what love was, she knew now. Not pretense or deception, not just pleasing yourself. Love was more.

"You must go," she repeated. "Go and get well. For me."

Once, he had carried her off a battlefield. This time, she had to be the one who was strong. Everything inside her wanted to hold on to him, but she could not give in.

"Will you wait?" The pain in his eyes mirrored her own.

"Forever," she whispered. "Wherever you go, my love will be with you. When you have a place for me, I will come, God willing."

She bent and met his lips softly with her own, allowed the sweet touch to linger, tried to make this kiss one they would both remember through all the empty times ahead. When she straightened, she showed him the button, hanging on a ribbon around her neck. "I'll keep a little piece of you with me until you return."

"May I have a lock of your hair?"

She reached for the basket and found the small scissors she'd used to trim the cotton when she'd dressed his wound. She snipped a thick reddish brown curl and folded it within a clean handkerchief. He tucked it within his ragged jacket.

A trio of Confederate soldiers had come, ready to put Adam into the wagon, take him across the water, then to the train station and start him on his journey north. Elizabeth wished she'd begged permission to see him to the station, then changed her mind. This was agony enough.

Adam pressed her fingers one last time—would she ever feel his touch again? "Don't change, Elizabeth. I never want you to be less than yourself."

The men lifted him on his pallet. She was forced to step back. Tears stung behind her eyelids, but she blinked them away. She would weep later, when Adam was not there to see.

He turned his head for one last glimpse, whispered, "I love you."

They carried him out.

Elizabeth felt as if the sun had disappeared. Surely, the air had grown colder.

She felt Rosamund grip her arm, in comfort and support. "Have faith. The war will be over soon," her friend said.

Elizabeth shook her head. "I don't think so. I think it will be a long war, and hard."

Did she feel the premonition inside her, or was it only a reflection of her own pain?

"You'll find him again, you must! This is too unfair," Rosamund protested.

"Will I? How can we know."

Adam was out of sight. Elizabeth and Rosamund walked toward the gate, their shadows long against the prison walls. Now her tears fell in a steady stream, drowning her last vestiges of control. Wiping her wet cheeks uselessly, Elizabeth choked on a sob. She reached for the button on its ribbon and held it tight.

*Oh, Adam*, she thought. *I love you so. I will wait for you till the war ends, till the cannon fall silent, till we are no longer divided by battle lines.*

*Come back to me.*

A preview of the next Southern Angels novel: Winds
of Change

"Are you ready, *ma petite*?"

"Papa!" Victorine hurried to open her bedroom door. "Do you like my new gown?"

"*C'est belle, n'est-ce pas?*" Tante Marie waved her fan in excitement as she supervised her favorite niece's toilette. Tante Marie had been older than Victorine's maman, but she had the same gentle voice and kind heart as her dead sister. Victorine smiled at her aunt, then turned back to her father.

She whirled, enjoying the swish of silken petticoats and the heavier rustle of her brocade skirt. Her ball gown was a glorious sight, indeed. The crimson-hued brocade bodice was low-cut, trimmed and bound with gold embroidery. Her matching pelisse was lined with white ermine, with wide bands at the bottom.

Her maidservant Soozie stood back, a hairbrush in her coffee-colored hand, beaming with pride as her mistress displayed the result of their hours of preparation.

"You look like a princess." Monsieur LaGrande kissed her forehead lightly. "I missed you, *ma petite*, while you were away at school. This old house was very quiet. Look, I brought you something to wear tonight, at your first Mardi Gras ball."

For a moment, Victorine looked away. She'd tried to push back the memory of her ridiculous escapade of a week ago. Only her ankle's lingering soreness reminded her. Papa must never discover what had happened.

Now she focused on the black velvet box her father held out. When he flipped open the lid, she had no trouble forgetting her worries. She gasped. "Oh, Papa! *Tres jolies!*" She touched the ruby and diamond ear drops with one reverent finger.

"They were your maman's. I thought they would look very fine with your gown." Her father spoke softly.

Her aunt cooed over the jewelry, but Victorine's vision blurred as she remembered her gentle, beautiful mother, who had died too young of yellow fever. Determined not to be sad tonight, she blinked away the tears. "I will treasure them doubly."

She went back to her looking glass to position the earrings carefully. When she was done, Soozie held out her pelisse. Victorine slipped into it, then paused while her maid adjusted one strand of Victorine's dark hair.

"Such a shame your friend Colette took a chill and can't go tonight," her aunt murmured.

Victorine swallowed hard. "A pity," she agreed, accepting her father's arm. Tante Marie followed behind.

"I will escort the most beautiful lady at the ball," her father boasted, smiling. "The young men will be very jealous, *n'est pas*? There is one young man in particular that I want you to meet."

Blushing, Victorine knew her smile was wide. All her life she had waited for this moment, her first Mardi Gras ball. That prank a week ago didn't count, she told herself fiercely. Tonight she would walk in on her papa's arm, as she should, and meet the handsome prince she had always dreamed of. Her life was just beginning. The ball would be delightful, her life would be a series of happy events—surely the sadness was all behind her.

Victorine squeezed her father's arm. Then, balancing her heavy skirts, she walked slowly down the stairway.

When they entered the ballroom inside the house across town, Victorine paused while her father handed his top hat to the dark-skinned footman. She had already shed her pelisse, peeking into a looking glass to be sure that her elaborate hairdo was still perfect, while Tante Marie fussed with an errant curl.

The folding doors had been thrown back to combine the family's two parlors into one large salon for the party. Victorine glanced at the marble fireplace in the center of the wall, at the rosewood furniture, upholstered in expensive crimson silk. A crystal chandelier hung from the center of the ceiling, and the walls held oil paintings of generations of ancestors, tracing their host's Creole lineage back to the usual minor French aristocracy.

Victorine's heart beat rapidly. She could hear the rollicking music and the chatter of party-goers who already thronged the wide salon. She was glad that Creole ladies did not normally wear masks. She was too eager to see the ensemble to wish to peer through narrow eyeholes. Tonight, she wanted to see it all!

"You remember Mademoiselle Marie de Castillon, my late wife's sister, and my daughter Victorine LaGrande." Her father had paused to speak to a couple near the door, both gray-haired but very elegant in their dress.

She had not heard the rest of the introduction, but Victorine curtsied to the elderly couple.

"Ah, so nice to see you again, *ma cherie*," the woman said. "How you have grown! You look so much like your dear mother."

"*Merci, madam*," Victorine murmured. "That is praise, indeed."

"You must allow our son to have the pleasure of a dance. Where is that rascal?" She looked around the big ballroom.

But another couple was waiting behind them. Monsieur LaGrande shook his head.

"Bring him over when you find him, Louisa, we are holding up the latecomers."

He led Victorine and Tante Marie further into the room, and found narrow gilt chairs for them. Tante Marie settled herself comfortably and turned to gossip with the older lady sitting beside her.

But Victorine didn't want to sit down. The music was gay, and she found her foot tapping eagerly. The movement caused a twinge in her injured ankle. Despite herself she remembered the

American doctor's fingers probing it gently. His touch had been so warm and so strong. But that was another forbidden memory. Already there were couples moving smoothly on the dance floor. Would no one ask her to dance?

Her father smiled, as if reading her thoughts. "Would you allow your papa to have the first dance?"

"Oh, yes." Victorine flashed her father a wide smile, then followed him decorously onto the floor. As a child, she had watched her parents sway gracefully together. Her father was only about six inches taller than Victorine, and she could see the streaks of gray at his temples. They moved smoothly through the set, while the gas lights flickered against the gilt papered walls, and the perfumes of the dancers blended into a heady mixture of scent. She could feel the new ear drops gently brushing her neck as she glided across the hardwood floor. What a magical evening, Victorine thought.

When the tune ended, her father bowed to her and led her back to the edge of the dance floor.

"Rudolf," someone called to Monsieur LaGrande. An older man with a v-shaped beard approached.

"Excuse me for a moment, *ma petite,*" her father said.

Unwillingly, Victorine sat down on one of the narrow chairs, full skirts cascading around her. She was too impatient to sit still. Beneath her concealing hoop skirts, her feet mimicked the dance steps as the musicians struck up a new tune. She didn't want to waste a moment of this party.

"You look like a goddess of the night," a masculine voice said. "A wood nymph who has wandered into the city by chance. Can such beauty belong to a mortal girl?"

Startled, Victorine turned her gaze from the dance floor to find a slim young man of medium height standing beside her. His face looked familiar, and his smile was both lofty and intriguing.

"You are too kind," she said formally, remembering what her maman had taught her. "But we have not been introduced."

His dark eyes flashed, and the roguish smile curved even deeper.

"Do I need an introduction to a goddess? Shall I not bow in humble subjection to your beauty, instead? Or throw myself into the sea in sacrifice if you choose not to smile upon me?" "Silly," Victorine murmured, but she flushed at the

outrageous compliments. Then a memory reappeared, and she held her breath. This was the striking young man she had glimpsed at the secret ball, the one with the beautiful girl on his arm. She looked away, gripping her fan so tightly that she heard a delicate ivory rib crack.

She heard the puzzlement in his voice. "Have I offended you? If so, I beg your pardon. But beauty can indeed overcome caution." His tone was low and persuasive. How could she explain the guilty secret that destroyed all her usual poise?

"No, no," Victorine muttered, shaking her head, but still not daring to look into his dark eyes.

"You see, I kneel before you, overcome with grief."

She couldn't help raising her gaze just a little. It was true. He knelt on the wood floor, to the detriment of his expensive trousers.

She blushed again. People were already staring. "*Mais non*, do get up," she begged. "The gossip—we will be laughed at. Get up at once, *s'il vous plait*."

He rose, but she saw the flash of quick anger in his expression. "Non, non, my wood nymph. No one would dare to laugh. The ruffian would receive my challenge before he had closed his mouth, and we would meet at dawn beneath the dueling oaks. And he would never laugh again!"

A duel? Victorine opened her eyes wide. Throughout her childhood, she had heard endless gossip of hot-blooded encounters in the Crescent City.

He took her hand and pressed it between his own. "Do not look so alarmed, little nymph. No one would dare to offend me. My reputation with the sword is too great."

She could feel the warmth of his hand through the thin gloves, and her own heart beating faster. Was this the handsome prince she had always dreamed of—this dashing young stranger with his outrageous remarks? Had she walked into her fantasy?

In her daydreams, she would have flirted back, said exactly the right thing to captivate a worldly young man. But the memory of the forbidden ball slowed her thoughts, and her usual ready answer had disappeared. She looked down at her small hand still gripped firmly in both of his and was silent.

"Still worried about the lack of formal introduction, *ma belle*? Shall I remedy this small omission?" His tone was laughing again. She felt young and foolish.

"*Voila*! There you are, Andre, and you have already met the lovely Victorine?" The elegant gray-haired lady who had spoken earlier to Victorine and her father sailed up, her lavender dress with its hoop skirts as majestic as a clipper ship gliding over a smooth sea.

"Indeed, I could not miss the most beautiful lady at the ball," Andre agreed, his tone almost too formal. Was he laughing at her, a little?

But Victorine's doubt disappeared as the introduction was performed. "My son, the redoubtable Andre Valmont," his mother said, her tone wry. "Make your bow to Mademoiselle LaGrande."

Valmont? *This* was the young man about whom her papa had hinted? Victorine blinked, then tried not to smile. She could tell Madam Valmont that her son had already been on his knees to her, but she blushed at even considering such a bold statement, true though it was. And how foolish she had been, objecting to the attentions of the most eligible bachelor at the party. The

Valmonts were old friends of her parents, and their wealth and social prestige in the Creole community rivaled her own family's. Her father had left his conversation and hurried to rejoin them. "I see you have found your missing heir," Monsieur LaGrande said to Madam Valmont, smiling. "Have you met my daughter, then, Andre?"

"It is my great pleasure," Andre agreed. "But I should be even happier if she would allow me the honor of a dance."

"*Bien sur*," Monsieur LaGrande agreed, before Victorine had time to answer. To his daughter, he said, "You will find Andre a most accomplished dancer, *ma petite*."

Her cheeks still hot, Victorine simply nodded and allowed Andre to escort her onto the dance floor.

"Happy, now, *ma belle?*" Andre murmured, bowing over her hand.

Victorine smiled briefly and did not answer as they glided through the intricate pattern of the dance. Andre was, indeed, a polished dancer, and she must not look clumsy in comparison. Not until the music died did she look up into his dark eyes again. She detected a gleam of mischief there.

"You are as graceful as you are beautiful, my wood nymph. Would you care to stroll in the courtyard?"

"Perhaps. But do you expect me to turn into a tree?" Victorine fluttered her dark lashes, flipping open her fan. She would not allow him to see that the thought of being alone in the darkness with this young gallant made her stomach tighten. Despite her papa's approval, despite her own racing pulse, she would not make Andre Valmont's courtship too simple a task.

Andre blinked, then laughed aloud. "Your beauty is such that you hardly seem mortal, Mademoiselle. I would not be surprised to see you sprout leaves."

"To avoid your pursuit?" Victorine raised her fan to hide her smile. "I trust you will give me no reason to do so?"

"No indeed," Andre said quickly. "You are safe with me, always." Then his dark eyes sparkled as he detected the smile she didn't quite hide. "You rogue, you make sport of me! Come, we shall walk in the courtyard."

Picking up her skirts with one hand, she laid the other in the curve of his arm. As they walked through the open veranda doors, she saw several couples enjoying the moonlight, and a matron or two to chaperon.

Lush potted plants framed the brick courtyard, and the air was heavy with moisture. The faint breath of a breeze cooled Victorine's cheeks and bare shoulders. Green vines encircled the white pillars of the piazza and made lacy patterns on the walls of the house, while green window shutters stood open to catch the air. The large leaves of a banana tree fluttered, and a fountain splashed merrily in the center. Flower beds edged the wall. Andre nodded toward a bench. "Shall we sit?"

Victorine had been enjoying the cool air, but now she lifted her brows. "I should not linger too long without my aunt or papa," she demurred. This was not Charleston, she must remember. Creole girls were strictly chaperoned at all times.

"I think your papa would be pleased at anything we did," Andre argued, a gleam in his dark eyes. "But I will not distress you. You are young yet, and innocent, as it should be."

Victorine frowned. She was seventeen, after all, a

young lady. "I am not distressed," she declared flatly. Holding her head high, she walked across the brick courtyard and sank gracefully to the bench.

Victorine saw a couple leaning close together. The

young man whispering to his sweetheart brought another thought to her mind.

"Andre, that gentleman is in uniform. Are many men here signing up for service to our Southern forces, the Confederacy?"

Andre shrugged. "*Mais oui*, it's all the rage, these volunteer companies. But a waste of time, really. The Yankees will never take New Orleans."

"He looks very fine," Victorine murmured, using her fan skillfully.

Andre had lost his smile. "His trousers do not hang well," he pointed out. "And his jacket is too tight across the shoulders."

Victorine refused to be distracted by the fit of the young man's uniform. "But so brave! One must admire their courage. I saw Fort Sumter bombarded from the windows of my school, did you know, when the great war began."

"No place for a lady to be," Andre objected. "Were you not frightened?"

"Oh yes. We could feel the school house shake." Victorine shivered, just remembering. "My friends climbed out on the roof to watch, but I could not bear to stay."

"*Mon dieu*, I should think not." Andre nodded approval. "Who expects a lady to show courage? That is for men."

But to her surprise, Victorine felt a flicker of annoyance. Don't I have the right to support my homeland? she thought. Still a lady did not argue with a gentleman.

"Southern ladies are to be protected, adored," Andre was explaining. "My wife—she will be the most pampered of creatures, as it should be, *non*?"

The thought—the merest suggestion—of being the wife of the handsome and dashing Andre Valmont was enough to make Victorine forget everything else. She felt her cheeks go hot, and she stared down at the bricks beneath her feet.

Andre's voice was gentle, now. He reached to take her hand. "Have I frightened you, *ma petite*? Do not be alarmed. Would it be such a dreadful fate, to be Madam Andre Valmont?"

"*Non, non*," Victorine murmured, very conscious of the gentle pressure of his hand. She could not meet his gaze. He was so handsome that her thoughts scattered every time she looked into those liquid dark eyes. But this was so soon for words of love. Trying to gauge his sincerity, Victorine looked up.

His dark eyes met hers without the twinkle of mischief she sometimes glimpsed there. He raised her hand to his lips, kissing her gloved fingers lightly.

"You are so beautiful, little Victorine, that any man would kneel at your feet. I shall need all of my skill as a swordsman to fight off your other suitors."

Her head swam as he kissed her hand, pressing her fingers lightly. She felt a quivering in her stomach, and her heart beat very fast. She had dreamed of this for years, her first romance, her first love, but the truth seemed more exciting than she had ever imagined. The courtyard around them seemed hazy in the flickering light. Victorine would not have been surprised to see a fairy godmother smiling at her from behind a magnolia tree.

If this were a dream, Victorine hoped she would never wake. And yet, she had been flirted with before. There had been young men in Charleston, at teas and parties, who had also made pretty speeches. How much did his compliments mean? Was Monsieur Valmont in earnest?

Andre smiled, and Victorine tried to think of a reply. She mustn't let him see that he left her weak.

"Your words are sweet, Monsieur Valmont," she said softly. "Is your heart as true as your words are polished?" Andre's dark eyes flashed. Victorine held her breath. "You doubt the worth of my affections? *Mais non*, Mademoiselle, you shall see what is to be courted by Andre Valmont."

As if his statement alone were not enough to make her breath come fast, he leaned forward. Victorine's eyes widened.

He lifted her hand again and this time turned her hand to kiss her gloved palm. Even through her thin gloves, the warm pressure of his lips made her tremble. His dark lashes were long and thick, and his lips were smooth—how would it be to kiss such a man? It was a daring thought. Victorine shivered again.

"Is it too cool for you?" Andre asked. "We will go in. But do not forget, my heart is not given lightly, *ma belle*. We will talk of this again. For now, may I have the honor of another dance?" Victorine nodded. The gay music drifted out to the courtyard, and she was happy to rejoin the light and bustle of the crowded ballroom. To sway lightly in Andre's practiced grasp, one hand holding hers, the other at her waist, guiding her through the steps—what bliss.

Was this what marriage to Andre Valmont would be like, to have his hand guiding her, his arm always protecting her? Her head whirled at the thought, and her heart seemed to be in her throat.

The music played on, and Victorine floated on a cloud of happiness. She danced with the most handsome man in the room, and he had eyes only for her. She could almost believe that Andre loved her already, despite the fact that they had just met. The tight knot of excitement inside her seemed to grow until she felt overcome with happiness, drowned in joy. She hoped the night would never end.

Other young men clustered around her, begging for a dance, but she hardly saw them. Andre alone made the room brighter, the music sweeter.

Later, when Andre had bowed over her hand one last time, and her papa had escorted her and her aunt home, she entered their front door still feeling dazed.

"Our Victorine was the most beautiful young lady of all," Tante Marie declared fondly.

"Was the ball all you thought it would be?" her father asked.

Victorine nodded, smiling a secret smile. She felt just like Cinderella, except she had not lost her glass slipper, and her happiness had no dark threat to mar it.

Then she remembered the secret ball, the dark-haired beauty on Andre's arm who had looked up at him with such trust. For a moment, her contentment vanished. Had Andre said the same sweet words to that other girl?

Surely not! Just because he had danced with her, smiled and laughed, it meant nothing. A party flirtation, that was all. If he hinted of marriage to Victorine, it must mean that his heart was not engaged elsewhere.

Victorine pushed any doubts away. She had found her prince, and he was as handsome and distinguished as any romantic young lady could wish. Nothing would spoil her new-found happiness.

Nothing!

Cheryl Zach has published around 50 novels, mainly for young adult and adult readers, with major New York publishers. Some were best sellers and most were critically acclaimed. She is the only author for Young Adults to be inducted into the Romance Writers of America Hall of Fame. She loves history, adventure, mystery, and fantasy, and reading in general. Born in Tennessee into a military family, she changed schools ten times in twelve years. She has also lived in Kentucky, Georgia, Texas, on the Mississippi Gulf Coast, in southern California, and in Britain and Germany. She has visited most of the other states and several other foreign countries. She was a National Merit Scholarship winner and has a B.A. and M.A. in English. She speaks at writing conferences and schools around the nation.

Her website is www.cherylzach.com and she blogs at kidsbookmavens.com

Virginian Elizabeth Stafford finds increased freedom at a boarding school in Charleston, S.C. She has new friends and handsome young men courting her. When she meets Union officer Adam Cranfield, her life could change even more. But South Carolina secedes, and she can't marry a Yankee. Even if the country is divided, who will tell her heart it must not cross the line?

Come with Elizabeth, Victorine, Hannah, and Rosamund as they confront America's most turbulent era. Can they stay friends as loyalties are torn asunder? And can they find true love amid the uncertainty and dangers of wartime?

Hearts Divided is a Virginia Romance Writers Holt Medallion winner.

# Don't miss out!

Click the button below and you can sign up to receive emails whenever Cheryl Zach publishes a new book. There's no charge and no obligation.

Did you love *Hearts Divided*? Then you should read *Winds of Change* by Cheryl Zach!

Victorine LaGrande returns to her home in New Orleans to prepare for marriage. But the handsome Creole 'prince charming' her father has chosen to be her husband is in love with another woman. Will she fight for his love, with the help of a Voodoo queen's love potion? Or will Victorine yield to her attraction to the off limits young American doctor, who needs her help when she must flee from General 'Beast' Butler after Union forces occupy her beloved city?

52219990R00115

Made in the USA
Lexington, KY
21 May 2016